*S...*
*wh...*

She couldn't remember too much after glass number five. She most certainly did not remember how she ended up in a room she obviously shared with the person in the shower.

She combed her fingers through her long sable-colored hair at the same time that the bathroom door opened. She almost scrambled under the bed. Instead, she grabbed the hem of the sheet and yanked it up to her neck.

And just in time, too. As a nearly naked Gerrick stepped around the bathroom door, Gina's heart almost stopped....

Dear Reader,

We have some incredibly fun and romantic Silhouette Romance titles for you this July. But as excited as we are about them, we also want to hear from *you!* Drop us a note—or visit www.eHarlequin.com—and tell us which stories you enjoyed the most, and what you'd like to see from us in the future.

We know you love emotion-packed romances, so don't miss Cara Colter's CROWN AND GLORY cross-line series installment, *Her Royal Husband*. Jordan Ashbury had no idea the man who'd fathered her child was a prince—until she reported for duty at his palace! Carla Cassidy spins an enchanting yarn in *More Than Meets the Eye*, the first of our A TALE OF THE SEA, the must-read Silhouette Romance miniseries about four very special siblings.

The temperature's rising not just outdoors, but also in Susan Meier's *Married in the Morning*. If the ring on her finger and the Vegas hotel room were any clue, Gina Martin was now the wife of Gerrick Green! Then jump into Lilian Darcy's tender *Pregnant and Protected*, about a fiery heiress who falls for her bodyguard....

Rounding out the month, Gail Martin crafts a fun, lighthearted tale about two former high school enemies in *Let's Pretend*.... And we're especially delighted to welcome new author Betsy Eliot's *The Brain & the Beauty*, about a young mother who braves a grumpy recluse in his dark tower.

Happy reading—and please keep in touch!

*Mary-Theresa Hussey*

Mary-Theresa Hussey
Senior Editor

# Married in the Morning

## SUSAN MEIER

*SILHOUETTE* *Romance*®

Published by Silhouette Books

America's Publisher of Contemporary Romance

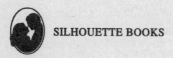 

SILHOUETTE BOOKS

ISBN 0-373-19601-6

MARRIED IN THE MORNING

Copyright © 2002 by Linda Susan Meier

Visit Silhouette at www.eHarlequin.com

**Printed in U.S.A.**

## SUSAN MEIER

is one of eleven children, and though she has yet to write a book about a big family, many of her books explore the dynamics of "unusual" family situations, such as large work "families," bosses who behave like overprotective fathers or "sister" bonds created between friends. Because she has more than twenty nieces and nephews, children also are always popping up in her stories. Many of the funny scenes in her books are based on experiences raising her own children or interacting with her nieces and nephews.

She was born and raised in western Pennsylvania and continues to live in Pennsylvania.

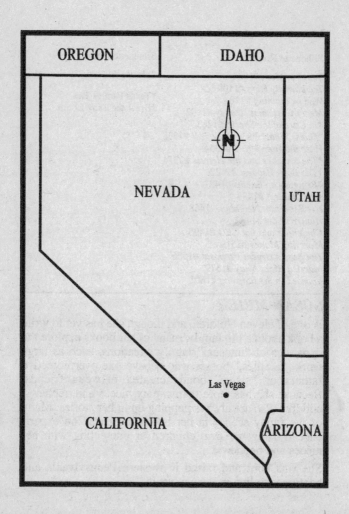

# Chapter One

Gina Martin awakened to the sound of the shower. Cool, satiny sheets caressed her bare limbs. The room smelled of cinnamon.

*Cinnamon?*

Her eyes sprang open, causing a spasm of pain to ricochet around inside her head, and she snapped them closed again. But not before she saw that she wasn't in her bedroom. From the type of furniture and shape and style of the room, she knew she was in a hotel.

She was in a hotel.

Someone was in the shower.

She was naked.

*Oh...*

*My...*

*Lord.*

Odd images floated around in her brain...

She and Gerrick Green, a vice president in her family's grocery store conglomerate, Hilton-Cooper-Martin Foods, had met unexpectedly at a small neighborhood bar, where each was supposed to be joining a friend for dinner....

Enough time had passed for both to realize they had been stood up. She by her friend Tammy. Gerrick by a married friend who was going to help him celebrate his new job. Until that moment Gina hadn't known Gerrick had gotten a new job, but he had happily filled her in. He had been offered the position as CEO of an up-and-coming grocery store chain in the northeast and had already turned in his two-week notice to her father.

Though she was director of Human Resources at Hilton-Cooper-Martin Foods and therefore the person who would have to replace him, Gina was happy for Gerrick. She remembered suggesting she celebrate with him since they were both unexpectedly free. She remembered he was reluctant. She remembered telling him this job was an enormous step on the ladder because it meant he had "made it." And she couldn't let a promotion so significant occur without at least some pomp and circumstance.

She remembered Gerrick finally laughing and relenting, saying this kind of job did warrant a celebration.

She remembered Gerrick taking her hand because, much to her surprise, he hadn't wanted to stay in the small neighborhood bar where they'd met. Laughing, holding her hand, he had whisked her into a cab and to the airport for a flight to Las Vegas because he said Vegas was where the best celebrating was done.

And he was right. The city was delightfully hedonistic and decadent, and it offered celebration possibilities a person couldn't get anywhere else. Because of the time difference from Atlanta, they arrived at about the same time they left, had dinner and saw a show before they went to separate rooms. Saturday morning they shopped for two days' worth of clothes, returned to their rooms to change into one of their clean outfits and went sight-seeing.

But Saturday afternoon—yesterday afternoon—they hit the casino. Specifically, Gina remembered falling in love with the poker game on the slots. As she recalled, she was winning. Not just winning, but annihilating every machine she touched. They moved on to the blackjack tables and her luck held, so they never left the casino. She remembered laughing and virtually dancing for joy over her good fortune. She remembered Gerrick stealing a kiss that startled her because it was a real kiss. Not just a peck between friends, but an honest-to-goodness kiss full of passion and promise. She remembered a waitress who brought glass after glass of champagne....

Oh, boy.

She *couldn't* remember eating dinner. She couldn't remember too much after glass number five of champagne. She most certainly did not remember how she ended up in a room that she obviously shared with the person taking a shower.

She didn't even really know for sure who the showering person was...though she could make a darned good guess.

She combed her fingers through her long sable-colored hair at the same time that the bathroom door opened. She almost scrambled under the bed. Instead, she grabbed the hem of the sheet and yanked it up to her neck.

Just in time. Gerrick rounded the corner and Gina's heart stopped.

Wrapped in a white hotel towel with his black hair still wet from the recent washing, he didn't have an ounce of modesty or regret. His green eyes twinkled with happiness. Unable to hold his gaze, Gina averted hers only to find herself looking at the well-defined muscles of his arms and chest. Dark hair dusted his pectorals and rippled down his flat stomach.

Embarrassment overwhelmed her, but she didn't get the chance to wallow in it. Gerrick walked to her side of the bed, bent down and took her by the shoulders, lifting her up for a long, wet kiss. As his mouth plundered hers, millions of sensations bounced through her. Everything from unexpected pleasure to complete shock. She smelled the soap from his shower, tasted pure passion in his kiss and her arms grew so weak they sort of fell against her sides and the sheet slid away from her.

Gerrick raised her higher, nestling her breasts against his still damp chest and Gina felt the beginnings of hyperventilation welling up in her lungs. Then he let her drift back down to the bed, but when she was settled, he held her face with his big, strong hands, and gazed into her eyes.

"Good morning."

Gina swallowed. "Good morning," she said, surprised not only by the sexy huskiness of her own voice, but also the warm affection in his. If she were a betting woman, and after yesterday it was plain she was, she would guess that this man didn't just like her, he adored her.

Still smiling at her, he stepped away. "Give me your room key and after I dress I'll go and get the clothes you bought at the hotel store to wear home. Our flight leaves in three hours, but we should be at the airport at least two hours beforehand. In fact, I thought we'd grab breakfast there after we check in."

While he spoke, Gina continued piecing things together. Her clean clothes were in another room. He had been gentleman enough to offer to retrieve them for her, but if she went she could get time away from him. Time to think this through. Time to figure out what had happened and how she'd ended up in this room, with this man, doing who only knew what.

"How about if I just go to my room and get dressed?" she asked, struggling not to insult him or embarrass herself by sounding foolish and nervous. "This way we won't fight over who gets the mirror in the bathroom first."

He laughed heartily. "We're allowed to use the bathroom at the same time now."

"Don't be silly." She shifted slightly to get out of bed, but remembered she was naked. Obviously they had made love the night before, but in the light of day and cold sober she didn't feel like prancing around in front of him. She gingerly slid back to her original position. "You're not dressed yet, and I can throw on my clothes from yesterday, go to my room, get myself showered and dressed and meet you in the lobby in less than an hour. That way we'll have plenty of time for breakfast at the airport."

"You're sure?"

"Yeah. Absolutely," she said, amazed at how calm, casual and even sophisticated she sounded. "You go ahead and get ready and I'll meet you in the lobby as soon as I can."

She said the last assuming he would return to the bathroom. God only knew why. Instead he dropped his towel and walked to the closet. Her heart stopped again, and her mouth fell open because he was gorgeous. His shoulders were broad. His butt was tight. The muscles of his legs were well defined. In short he was perfect.

However, he also wasn't shy about being naked in front of her and he apparently didn't expect her to be shy about being naked in front of him.

Okay. Now what?

Planning the fastest way to get dressed, Gina quickly glanced around to locate her clothes. Red sandals sat by the door. A red blouse perched over the back of a chair. A pair of taupe slacks lay in a puddle on the floor. A red bra was…oh, boy…slung across a lamp. Bright red panties hung from the pleat of a curtain. Whatever they had done the night before it had to have been…well, wild. She managed to suppress the shiver that wanted to race through her, but couldn't stop herself from swallowing. Not only were the red bra and panties more than out of character for her, but she couldn't remember how her underwear got caught on a curtain.

Deciding that the cool, calm, collected charade was impossible to continue, she dragged the sheet from the bed and wrapped it around herself before she walked to the lamp and grabbed her bra. She saw Gerrick watching her reflection in the mirror, but paid no attention as she snatched up her blouse and slacks. Unfortunately, when she walked to the window and peered up at her panties, which were really more like two scraps of lace, looped over a curtain pleat, she realized she couldn't reach them.

A little voice told her that for the five minutes it would take her to go to her room, she could forgo the underwear. She was just about to listen to that sage advice when Gerrick ambled over to the window, reached up to retrieve the scraps of red lace and handed them to her with a smile.

The heat of embarrassment shivered through her. Mortification froze her lungs. But Gerrick dropped a quick kiss on her lips as she took the panties. Then he mercifully disappeared behind the bathroom door.

Gina heaved a sigh of relief and dressed faster than she had ever dressed in her entire life. She found a little red clutch bag, assumed it was hers and rifled through it finding both her wallet and room key. But as she rummaged a flash hit her eyes and she felt an unusual weight on the third finger of her left hand. She flipped the purse over so quickly, most of the contents spilled onto the floor, and when she saw the three-diamond wedding band on her finger she fell to the bed. Literally. Her knees buckled and her muscles grew limp. She was lucky to be standing beside something that could catch her.

She hadn't just slept with Gerrick Green. It appeared she had married him.

Not wasting another second, Gina scooped up the contents of her purse and raced out the door. In the elevator, she tapped her foot as the car ascended to her floor. She shoved the key card into the door of her room, stripped even faster than she had dressed and jumped into the shower.

With the water noisily tumbling around her, beating off the tile walls and porcelain tub, she let herself scream.

"Hi."

"Hi."

As Gina said her greeting, Gerrick slid his arm around her waist and pulled her to him so he could kiss her, confirming the only solid conclusion she had drawn sorting through this mess.

Gerrick was not sorry they had slept together, and he was not sorry they had married. He probably did not know she didn't remember marrying him or making love. And she didn't know how she was going to get out of this situation gracefully.

She didn't know if she *could* get out of it gracefully.

"Let's get a cab," Gerrick said, taking the tote bag she had purchased to carry home her changes of clothes and new toiletries, and ushering her through the hotel casino and registration area and into the hot Las Vegas sun.

A line of taxis sat waiting and Gerrick and Gina were directed to the first one by the doorman. Gerrick pushed their two small bags onto the back seat of the cab, helped Gina in, and then tipped the doorman before sliding in beside her.

Gina smiled at him, but the hotel they had chosen was less than fifteen minutes away from the airport and she needed more time to think. So she turned her face to the window as if she was sight-seeing and began processing the facts.

She met Gerrick when she was sixteen. He was twenty-two, fresh out of college and going to work for her dad. She, of course, thought he was cute. No self-respecting sixteen-year-old could not think he was cute. He was the epitome of tall, dark and handsome. But he was also six years older than she was. An important six years since he was an adult and she was still a schoolgirl. And that had been the end of that.

At twenty-two she had joined her father's company. She was immediately put on the executive fast track, because she was the daughter of the chairman of the board and majority shareholder, and therefore the person most likely to take over someday. A few of the other executives had resented her. Gerrick had welcomed her. For that she had immediately liked him. But she also knew she would someday be his boss, so she kept her distance.

So had he.

Over the past six years they had worked together, exchanged pleasantries about weekends and vacations, but never shared a long, detailed personal conversation until Friday night.

And now they were married.

Surprisingly, part of her wasn't sorry. First, she was attracted to him. Second, he was a good person. She had known him for twelve years. In that twelve years he had proven himself to be generous, honest and hardworking.

And she liked him. She had *always* liked him.

Silly as it sounded, she could become a giddy bride with only the slightest push.

Gerrick took her hand, squeezed lightly and smiled at her, and Gina felt herself tumbling over the edge into giddiness.

Could she do this?

Could she be a bubbling bride with a man she didn't really know, but with whom she was clearly infatuated?

Oh, God, she wanted to! She wanted it so much it scared her.

They arrived at the airport, checked in and immediately found a restaurant. The entire time Gerrick held her hand. She felt young and beautiful and on the verge of a brand new life with a wonderful man. For the first time since her fiancé Chad had dumped her the year before, she felt happy.... No, what she felt was hopeful. Life had meaning and purpose again. She had things to do other than be Hilton Martin's daughter.

"Okay," Gerrick said the very second their waitress served their breakfasts and indicated she would let them alone unless they waved her over. "I think we have some talking to do."

"Yeah, I guess we do," Gina said, still not sure how to handle this. Even if she decided to stay married, she knew she would have to confess that she didn't remember getting married or making love. That was the fair, appropriate thing to do. And, once she confessed that she didn't remember making love or getting married, Gerrick might not want to stay married to her. Which effectively took the decision out of her hands, and also saddened her. If she told him she didn't remember marrying him or making love and he told her that he couldn't stay married to a woman who hadn't made a real commitment, then all this wonderful fun would be over.

Still, she had to do the right thing.

"Gerrick, I don't know how to tell you this but..."

"The first thing we need to discuss is how we get you from Atlanta to Maine in less than two weeks."

"Excuse me?" Though they had spoken at the same time, Gina hadn't missed what Gerrick said. It awakened her like a glass of water splashed into the face of a sleeping person, and her eyes widened.

"Gina, you can't stay in Atlanta if you're married to a man who lives in Maine," Gerrick said, with a chuckle.

Gina sat back on her seat. Okay. Here was reason number one why their being married might not work. She had spent her life being groomed to take over her family's company. In her head, she saw herself as an executive. Now, she was an executive's wife. She didn't know if it was a promotion or a demotion. She didn't know if she liked it. She didn't even know if she could do it.

"You're still going to Maine?" she asked.

"This job is the biggest thing that's ever happened to me. I can't turn it down."

"Some people might think getting married is the biggest thing that ever happened to you...."

Gerrick reached across the table, took her hand, brought it to his lips and kissed it. "They would be right."

*Oh, boy.* The pit of her stomach went soft again. Tears filled her eyes. He was so darned romantic. He even looked romantic. His dark eyes were warm with affection. His beautiful mouth held just the hint of a smile. Wearing jeans and a simple polo shirt he should have looked rumpled and unkempt. Instead, he just looked cute.

How could she give him up?

"So maybe then it would be appropriate to absorb one big change before making another?"

"Don't be silly. We're two of the smartest people I know. We can handle this transition in our sleep."

It bowled her over that he so easily, so casually called her smart. A lot of people believed she was only in her job because of her family status. Hearing Gerrick acknowledge her intelligence and readily accept it proved he knew more about her than the simple surface things everyone else saw or assumed.

She licked her dry lips. He seemed so sure, so happy. He seemed to know her. He seemed to *love* her. His love made her long for things she never thought she would have and made her eager to abandon everything for the chance to grab the life he could give her.

"But I have family responsibilities."

He looked her right in the eye. "Do you?"

She wasn't a hundred percent sure what he was asking, but if he was hinting at what she suspected he was hinting at, she needed time to think about that, too.

Luckily, he smiled. "You know what? I think we've just jumped into the 'too much too soon' category. So what do you say we enjoy our breakfast, enjoy our flight and then talk when we get home?"

Because that sounded very good to her, Gina nodded. She had never been so confused in her entire life, but one thing was clear. Gerrick Green knew her. He anticipated her moods. He didn't push too hard or too far. He respected her. Somehow even tipsy—or maybe because she was in a freer, more open state of mind—she had recognized all this more quickly than in real time. And that was probably why she had married him.

They made small talk waiting for the plane, then chatted about inconsequential things during the flight, and it soon became evident to Gina that this man really did love her. She could see it in his eyes and hear it in his voice. She might not yet be able to say she "loved" him, but she knew him, respected him, liked him.

And something kept nudging her into believing that she shouldn't throw this away. Something was telling her that this was the chance of a lifetime. That if she didn't stay in this marriage she would miss out on a once-in-a-lifetime love.

By the time they reached Atlanta, she knew what she was going to do. Roll the dice. She wasn't sure how or why she had become such a gambler of late, but she had. She didn't have a clue how she would break this news to her father, but she was going to do that, too. She might be the person in line to replace him, but he was only in his late fifties. Nowhere near retirement. He was spirited enough and healthy enough to run this company for another fifteen or twenty years. By that time, she and Gerrick could have raised a family.

They disembarked and made their way to the row of taxis. This time when Gerrick kissed her, Gina kissed him back. She didn't merely allow her lips to slacken under his to accept his kiss. She returned his kiss, and when he caressed her lips with the tip of his tongue, she opened her mouth to him. She twined her tongue with his, enjoying every exquisite sensation, almost unable to believe that this wonderful man was hers, but more than willing to accept it as yet another stroke of the good luck she had acquired in Vegas.

And Gerrick almost relaxed. Almost, but not quite. He hadn't exactly tricked Gina into marrying him, but he hadn't let the opportunity pass him by, either. When she proposed, he jumped on it, ushering her to the hotel chapel where they found an official who was in between services and more than happy to perform their ceremony. The waitress who had been providing their champagne and to whom Gina had given a three-hundred-dollar tip was thrilled to be her maid of honor. One of their blackjack dealers acted as Gerrick's best man. It was the most important, most exciting moment of his life, but he wasn't so dumb as to miss that in the light of day, Gina was having second thoughts.

He could handle that. He might have been head over heels in love with her for the past few months, but he recognized all this was new for her because until this weekend she had been at the very end of getting over her last romance. In fact, his feelings for her began with his worry over her upset about the man who had thrown her over for a co-ed with whom he was having an affair. That caused Gerrick to make time to talk to her every morning, eat lunch with her at least once a week and walk her to her office after meetings. Ultimately, concern grew into genuine affection, and before he knew it he found himself absolutely crazy about her. But he didn't think Gina had noticed him as anything other than a co-worker at Hilton-Cooper-Martin Foods until Friday night. Still, once she had begun the process of seeing him as a person, a man, she seemed to catch up to his level of feelings with leaps and bounds.

And besides, she was the one who proposed to him.

Plus, he was leaving Atlanta in two weeks. Unless he married her he had no way of coercing her into moving with him, and no reason really to even keep in touch, except that they had had a fun time gambling in Vegas. That wasn't much of a foot in the door and in his mind the marriage was a necessity.

On the flight home, the time difference worked against them, and it was already late afternoon when they arrived. They took a taxi to the bar where they had met on Friday night and each drove his or her car to her father's mansion. She got there first, punched in the security codes that opened the big black gate and left it open. He drove through, then punched in the codes that locked the gate again. He wound his way up the long, tree-lined lane, taking his time, rehearsing in his head the speech he would give to his boss, searching for a way to describe their weekend without using the words tipsy or aroused. As he approached the house, he watched Gina pull her imported sports car behind the black sedan Gerrick recognized as belonging to Ethan McKenzie, head of the Legal Department of Hilton-Cooper-Martin Foods and family friend of Hilton Martin.

Great. That meant they might have to wait hours before they actually told Hilton they were married.

Gerrick groaned. No, they wouldn't. He had bought Gina a platinum band with three one-karat marquise diamonds. Nobody was going to miss that. Especially not eagle-eyed Ethan. They weren't going to get to announce this to Hilton privately unless Gerrick did something fast.

He jumped out of his car and rushed toward the front entrance attempting to get to Gina before she walked in and flashed her ring, but he was too late. As if he had been waiting for Gina, Ethan opened the door and plowed forward before she reached for the knob. He took her by the shoulders and, if the look on his face was anything to go by, said something very serious to her.

Gerrick saw Gina gasp and crumple in Ethan's arms, then both Gina and Ethan scrambled from the doorway to Ethan's car.

Approaching from the other side, Gerrick was almost to the doorstep when they dashed away, ignoring him as if he wasn't there.

He stopped.

Ethan drove up beside him, and lowered his car window. "Gerrick, I'm sorry. Hilton's had a heart attack. He was in Pennsylvania promoting a golf tournament he's helping to sponsor this summer. I've got Gina booked on the next flight out. Josh Anderson is already in Pennsylvania," he said, referring to Hilton-Cooper-Martin Food's PR director and Gina's cousin. Undoubtedly, Josh had been pressed into service as next of kin, since no one had known where Gina was. "Right now, we need somebody to hold down the fort. I think that should be you."

"Actually, Ethan," Gerrick said, glancing at Gina who was dabbing her eyes with a white tissue. "I think I should go with Gina to the hospital." He noticed the ring he had given her was conveniently hidden by her paper hanky and though that struck him as coincidentally lucky, he didn't question it.

Only now realizing they had been away together for the weekend, Ethan looked from one to the other then said, "Oh." He faced Gina again. "The second seat is booked in my name. Gerrick might not have time to get it changed and make the flight. We're late as it is."

"Then let's go," Gina said, urgency evident in her voice. "Gerrick, you're going to have to come up on a later flight."

"And I'll return home and hold the fort," Ethan said as he began to drive away.

Gerrick felt as if a truck had hit him. He had been employed by Hilton Martin his entire career. In some ways he loved Hilton like a father. That might even have been part of the reason he had been so casual about getting involved with Gina. But he also loved Gina. And he wanted to be with her. As her husband he *should* be the one with her. But Gina very clearly didn't want him. Or didn't care…

He was worried about Hilton. Fearful for Gina. Upset for himself. And insulted. But he ignored the stab of offense recognizing that Gina's first impulse was to get rid of him, not lean on him, because being offended had no place in a situation where a man's life hung in the balance.

Unfortunately, that still left him with intense worry, fear over Gina's pain and his own upset about Hilton. He didn't know which emotion to deal with first. So he got into his car and pulled out his cell phone to make reservations on the next available flight to Pittsburgh. Then he phoned Hilton's secretary to get directions to the hospital where Hilton was being treated. As he expected, Joanna had the information he needed.

Gerrick went home, packed a small suitcase, and drove back to the airport. Though his concern for Hilton was overwhelming, he couldn't help but remember the things he and Gina had done in this airport less than two hours ago. He saw the place where they had kissed. He saw the gate at which they had arrived laughing, full of happiness and hope. But when he walked down the tunnel to enter the plane, he also remembered that she had been having serious second thoughts during their flight home. It had taken hours to get her accustomed to the fact that they were married. And in seconds, in one announcement, they were back to square one.

He knew there was a very good possibility he would lose her tonight, if he didn't get to Johnstown, Pennsylvania before she completely changed her mind, succumbed to grief and fear and decided their marriage had been a mistake.

# Chapter Two

Gina didn't know who the woman in Vegas had been, but she did know it wasn't her. She was Gina Martin, daughter of Hilton Cooper Martin. She was destined to become CEO and chairman of the board of her family's grocery store conglomerate because she was the only child of the widower who had started the company and owned controlling interest in the stock. She didn't gamble. She didn't wear red bras and red lace thongs. She didn't marry a man on a whim, no matter how gorgeous. And her relatively young, very strong father did not have heart attacks.

As far as she was concerned, the entire universe had gone awry over the weekend and now she had to fix it.

Getting off the bone-jarring commuter flight she had taken to Johnstown, Pennsylvania, Gina slipped her three-karat diamond wedding ring into her trouser pocket, glad she had bought this pantsuit while shopping in Vegas. She not only had warm slacks and a blazer, but also a blouse. It wasn't much protection against the freezing temperatures of February in the Appalachian Mountains, but she was dressed warmer than Ethan was.

"The hospital is a short drive from here," Ethan said as they entered the rental car he had acquired at the one-man counter in the nothing-but-the-basics terminal. Wearing jeans and a T-shirt, dark-haired, dark-eyed Ethan looked like a man who had been unexpectedly yanked from enjoying a sunny Sunday afternoon with his wife and new son. He didn't even have a jacket. But worry about her father seemed to take precedence, because he made no comment about how cold it was. He simply started the car and turned on the heater.

"I got directions from the pilot."

Gina grimaced. "Small cities are awfully casual."

"But convenient." It was already close to eight, and it was dark. Ethan flicked on the headlights. "You probably couldn't get directions this good from anybody in Atlanta."

As if taking off her wedding ring had magically transformed her, Gina stopped agonizing over her foolish weekend. She knew she couldn't dwell on how stupid she had been or even how sick her father was. She had to get her mind in gear to make sure their company didn't fall apart in her dad's absence.

"So when Gerrick gets here you'll be going back?" she asked Ethan as he drove down a nearly empty four-lane highway.

"Yes, I think one of us has to be there."

She sighed. "No offense, Ethan, but you're in the Legal Department. You're not really up on the day-to-day business dealings."

"Then Josh Anderson's not a good choice to go home either, because he's our PR man," Ethan said, referring to Gina's cousin, the third person of the trio of Josh, Ethan and Gina, who were slated to take over the company when her father retired. Though Gina would be CEO and chairman of the board, it was already common knowledge that Josh would head Operations and Ethan would continue to lead the Legal Department. Because Hilton Martin was only in his fifties, and no one knew what role Gerrick would have played had he not left the company, her father had not begun transferring responsibilities or even training them for their future roles. Though Ethan could completely handle his own area of expertise, none of them could step into Hilton's shoes.

Particularly not Gina. It was her father's idea to put her in Human Resources so she could get to know all the employees and become familiar with their strengths and weaknesses. After that, she assumed he would begin showing her the ins and outs of the business in general. She even guessed that eventually she would move into an office by her dad, serve as his assistant and ultimately get the reins. But as of this time, all she had done was manage the employees.

"He might understand the stores," Ethan continued still talking about Josh. "But I don't think he can run them."

"So what we're saying is Gerrick needs to go home."

"He is vice president of Operations." Ethan sighed. "It's too bad we can't call him and tell him not to come up at all."

"He has to come up."

"Oh?" Ethan said, stealing a peek at her.

"Don't make a bigger deal out of this than it is," she said. Her business tone of voice came back so quickly and naturally that Gina was shocked she could have forgotten who she was for a second let alone an entire weekend.

Neither Gina nor Ethan said anything for the rest of the trip. He dropped her off at the sliding door entrance of the hospital, then drove away to find parking. She ran to the information desk, was given directions to the cardiac care floor, and proceeded to find her father. She knew Ethan would get the same information she had, the same way she had gotten it and wouldn't expect her to wait for him.

By the time Ethan arrived, Gina had been greeted by Josh and Olivia Brady—Josh's fiancée and one of Gina's best friends—had spoken to the doctor and was by her father's bed, where he lay sleeping. Because Ethan wasn't family, he wasn't allowed to come into the room. After her short visit was over, she joined Josh, Olivia and Ethan in the waiting room.

"Everything's going to be fine," Josh said immediately, while Olivia slid her arm around Gina's shoulders and helped her to a chair. Like Ethan, Olivia and Josh were dressed in jeans and simple T-shirts. Olivia's long blond hair was pulled into a bobbing ponytail. Josh's black hair was rumpled, as if he'd combed his fingers through it in frustration.

"Yeah, I know."

"And Ethan explained your plan about sending Gerrick home to run the company while you're up here."

"I think you all should go home."

"But…"

"No buts," Gina said, shaking her head. "I'm fine. But Dad's recovery will take weeks, and with all of us up here, the company will not be fine."

"The company will be fine without me," Olivia disagreed. "I quit last week, remember?"

"You quit to plan your wedding."

"Which is next month. Besides, everything's under control. I can spare some time away. Before you got here the doctor told us your dad could be transferred to a hospital in Atlanta as soon as he's able to travel. So it's not like you'll be here forever." She paused, caught Gina's gaze. "I'm staying."

Gina nodded. "Okay."

"Good," Olivia said, then removed her arm from around Gina's shoulders. "Now, when was the last time you ate?"

"Breakfast."

"You haven't eaten since breakfast!"

"Well, breakfast in Vegas was your lunchtime. So it wasn't that long ago."

"Vegas?" Ethan and Josh said simultaneously, before they exchanged a speculative look.

"Let's leave that alone," Gina said, then bit her quivering lip. For all her toughness about making sure the company would run smoothly, she suddenly wished Gerrick were here. But as quickly as she had the thought she stopped it. What they had done was wrong. Leaning on him was wrong. Leaning on *anybody* was wrong. She had to depend on people for business things, but that was simply letting them do their jobs. But she would not, could not, depend on anybody personally. She might not be in a position to take over this company today, or even next year, but by God she had to be someday and that meant she had to start being strong now.

Because there wasn't another direct flight to Pittsburgh, Gerrick had to endure a layover, then rent a car and drive from Pittsburgh to Johnstown. He didn't arrive at the hospital until almost midnight that night. When he stepped off the elevator onto the cardiac care floor, Gerrick didn't see Ethan McKenzie or Josh Anderson and assumed they were already on their way back to Atlanta. Olivia Brady, dressed in blue jeans and an old shirt, as if she'd dropped everything when she got the call about Hilton, was sleeping on a blue plastic sofa. Gina stood by a floor-to-ceiling window, gazing out at the lights of the city.

"I got here as soon as I could," Gerrick said, rushing over to Gina. He took her shoulders so he could turn her around and pull her into his arms. She accepted his comfort, but stiffly.

"Thank you, Gerrick, but I've thought this through…and talked about it with Josh and Ethan and you're actually the person who should be home, running the company."

"But I…"

"You're the only one of us who's in Operations. Actually, you're the only one of us who is a vice president. Josh and Ethan aren't that high on the corporate ladder yet, plus Ethan's in Legal and Josh is in Public Relations." She looked up at him, her pale-blue eyes blank and distant. "You're the only one who knows how to run the business."

Gerrick licked his dry lips. "Yes. You're right," he said, remembering that Olivia was in the room, remembering that they hadn't yet told anyone they had gotten married, and realizing that as they had never dated, the marriage would be as much of a shock to Olivia as Hilton's heart attack.

"How is your dad?"

"Resting."

Frustrated that they couldn't really talk, Gerrick glanced around. With the exception of sleeping Olivia, Gina and Gerrick had the huge waiting area, which was actually a wide corridor banked with chairs and fronted by little alcoves that also held chairs, all to themselves. He directed Gina to one of the cubbyholes and helped her sit. Continuing to hold her cold hands in his, he took the chair beside her.

"So, what's up?"

"Gerrick, I can't deal with this right now." She pulled her hands out of his, fished into her trouser pocket and retrieved his ring. She handed it to him.

Pain flooded Gerrick, but he ignored it. "I know," he said, taking the ring and sliding it into the pocket of his jeans. He didn't think she was breaking up with him, but giving him the ring for safekeeping. With three one-karat diamonds, it had been very expensive and it wasn't wise to have the ring rolling around in her pocket.

"So, I guess we'll talk when you get home."

Looking at her entwined fingers, she nodded. "The doctors say it will be at least a week before he can travel. I've made arrangements for a cardiologist friend of his to fly up from Atlanta tomorrow. He'll check Dad out and make a decision." She peeked up at him. "I won't know anything concrete until tomorrow."

He nodded.

"So there's no point in you hanging around."

"I can stay until…"

She shook her head. "I wish you wouldn't. Olivia's getting a hotel room and has agreed to keep me company. Josh and Ethan have already gone home." She paused, drew a quick breath. "It looks better this way."

"Your father and I are friends, Gina," Gerrick argued desperately. "Won't it look odd if I...?"

"Josh is my father's nephew and he's gone. It won't look odd if you return to Atlanta, but it will look odd if you insist on staying."

"Especially since I'm the one who should be at home minding the store," Gerrick conceded quietly because it was clear she wasn't going to budge, and he knew he had to let her handle things in the way that was easiest for her.

"Exactly."

"Okay," Gerrick said, rising. "Can I see him?"

She shook her head. "Only family can..."

"Gina, *I am* family."

Gina swallowed and nodded, then glanced over at Olivia, Gerrick guessed, to make sure she was still sleeping. Then she led him down the hall to the nurses' station and whispered that he was her husband and he would like to see her father. They were given orders to be out of the room in five minutes. When they slipped in, Gerrick got a full dose of seeing his idol, his mentor, his friend, attached to life support and breathing through tubes. Then he pressed his lips together and motioned to Gina to leave.

She nodded and followed him to the door.

"Walk me to the elevator?"

The relieved look on her face sent another shaft of pain through Gerrick, but again he ignored it. Seeing Hilton had impressed upon him that Gina had plenty to deal with handling the situation with her father. She shouldn't be sorting through the complications of an unexpected marriage, too. Yes, he knew that leaving her was risky. That she could talk herself out of their marriage in the few days they were apart. But if he didn't

leave, if he insisted on staying, if he insisted they announce this marriage, he would not only be an insen-
sitive clod, he knew with almost absolute certainty, the
marriage would be over.

He held Gina's hand as they walked to the elevator.
To an onlooker it was simply a friendly gesture, but
Gerrick realized how quickly, how easily he had fallen
into the role of her lover, her husband. They had been
romantically involved less than forty-eight hours, yet he
knew if he lost her it would kill him.

He pushed the elevator button and pulled her into his
arms. She came willingly, resting her head on his shoulder. So, he pressed his luck and gave her a soft kiss
before he stepped inside the car. She smiled briefly and
waved as the doors closed.

But Gerrick wasn't happy with the smile, or the
wave. Just like in their hotel room that morning in
Vegas, she hadn't kissed him back.

Gina took only one of Gerrick's calls in the days that
followed. In that conversation, she explained that because of the severity of her father's heart attack, Hilton's cardiologist friend had agreed that a catheterization should be done in the cardiac facility at the
Johnstown hospital rather than waiting until Hilton
could be moved to Atlanta. Josh and his mother, Hilton's sister, went to Pennsylvania to be with Gina during the procedure, which went very well. Josh returned
to work Friday reporting Hilton's prognosis was good.
He would be transferred to Atlanta in about a week, but
he would ultimately need bypass surgery.

With the news that Hilton was stable, Gerrick decided
to fly to Johnstown for the weekend. He didn't expect
Gina to announce their marriage, and he didn't plan to

play the role of husband. He just wanted to see her. He wanted to be sure she was okay. He wanted to be sure Hilton was okay. He wanted to do whatever he could because these people were his family. He felt it as surely as if he and Gina had dated for years instead of hours. And he couldn't stay away.

When he arrived in Hilton's private room, he found Gina and Hilton's friend, Dr. Brown, laughing and talking with a tired, but wide-awake Hilton Martin. His white hair was pillow-ruffled but his blue eyes were clear and bright.

"Gerrick, come in!" Hilton called as enthusiastically as an obviously weak man could. "Come in! What the devil possessed you to fly up here?"

"I came to see you," Gerrick said, smiling broadly with relief at seeing Hilton looking like he was on the road to recovery.

"And I'm fine. How's the company?"

"Uh-uh-uh…" Dr. Brown said, shaking his finger. "You don't get to talk business until after the bypass."

"Spoilsport!" Hilton said, but he laughed.

Gerrick's gaze drifted to Gina. Wearing blue jeans and a loose-knit hunter-green sweater that intensified the hue of her dark-brown hair, she couldn't have been prettier if she tried. Yet, something about her was off-kilter. She appeared pleased with her father's recovery, but she was different.

"Hi, Gina," Gerrick said, greeting her because he hadn't done so when he walked in.

"Hi, Gerrick."

Gerrick accepted her casual reply because of the circumstances and smiled, but Gina shifted her gaze away from him.

"Since Dr. Brown won't let me talk business," Hilton said, "I would feel much better, Gina, if you would go out into the hall and get the lowdown from Gerrick. So I'll know at least one of us is staying on top of things."

"There's really nothing pressing happening," Gerrick said, but Hilton waved him out. "You two go talk."

Because Hilton hadn't changed floors, only rooms, Gina and Gerrick returned to the corridor waiting area and the alcoves of chairs. They took seats in the first hideaway. It was private, but Gerrick nonetheless glanced around to see if he could do something as simple as take her hand.

Gina shook her head. "Don't."

"Don't?"

"Don't. I don't want you holding my hand."

"Gina, you don't have to worry," Gerrick said soothingly. "I'm not going to do anything to embarrass you or even announce our wedding. You're safe."

"I don't think so," Gina said, her voice barely a whisper. "Now that the worst is over and now that I've had time to think things through, I know I won't feel safe until we talk about our marriage."

"Okay. So, let's talk."

Gina straightened her shoulders and sat taller in her chair as if she were about to have a business discussion, not a personal one. She drew a long breath then said, "I had too much to drink the night we got married and I don't remember it. I don't remember if we consummated the marriage." Without so much as a blink, she steadily held his gaze. "I assume we did. But whatever happened, I don't remember and as far as I'm concerned that makes it a mistake."

"I disagree," Gerrick said calmly, though inside he

was reeling. *She didn't remember.* That would explain her hesitation when she awakened, and why she had second thoughts. But it didn't explain why she kissed him at the airport in Atlanta. Or the fact that she didn't want out of the marriage Sunday afternoon. Sunday afternoon she wanted to be his wife as much as he wanted to be her husband. Otherwise she wouldn't have let him come to her house, because she had to know the only reason for them to go to her father's home together was to tell him they were married.

"Gina, this just happened at a bad time. I'm willing to give you weeks or months to adjust if need be, but I don't think we made a mistake." He paused, took her hand. "I love you, Gina."

"You don't love me," Gina said, yanking her hand from his and shifting away from him, though she remained coolly detached. "We had a really great weekend but we do not love each other. Gerrick, I barely know you."

"We worked together for six years. We've known each other twelve."

She shook her head. "You don't really know the people you work with."

"Are you telling me you're hiding some deep, dark secret?"

"I'm telling you we made a mistake and I don't want to continue it. I want out." She combed her fingers through her thick brown hair, then shook her head in disgust. "I've got problems enough with my dad and I don't have the mental energy to argue with you. I don't even have time to be as diplomatic as I probably should be. And you don't, either. You've got a new job to go to."

"That's funny. Last week you were insisting only I

could stay behind to run the company in your father's absence. Now you want me to leave?''

''You *need* to leave. You need to get on with the rest of your life and I need to get on with mine.''

''I see,'' Gerrick said coolly and rose from his chair. Where had his wonderful Gina gone? Where was the sweet passionate woman who tormented him by fingering all the red and black lace bras in the hotel store? Where was the woman who made love with passion and abandon? Where was the woman who had asked him to marry her? ''I guess I should head for home, then.''

She nodded.

''I'll just say goodbye to your father.''

She nodded again. ''I'll be in in a minute.''

Gerrick took no comfort in the fact that Gina appeared to need to collect herself before returning to her father's room. Heeding doctor's orders, Gerrick also didn't tell Hilton that Gina had basically asked him to leave the company. He never lost his smile, his friendly demeanor, or even the spring in his step until he was boarding the commuter at Johnstown's airport, then he felt as if his entire world was crumbling around him.

He had loved her for months. Before he got the job offer in Maine he had been building up to asking her out by talking with her every chance he got. True, he hadn't told her about his family, but she knew as much as anybody knew about him personally. And he knew absolutely everything about her. Most of her growing-up years had been documented in the company's annual statement because it was a family-owned business. He knew her. He knew he loved her. And he knew that without her, his life would have almost no meaning.

His heart actually hurt, and he considered not leaving, waiting around until she came back and then trying to talk to her again. But Gina had made her wishes clear. She wouldn't be receptive to his staying. She wouldn't see his refusal to go as tenacity born of love. She would fight him tooth and nail, if only on principle. But more than that, if she didn't believe she knew him, if she had missed that he had been flirting with her for months, then she hadn't been paying any attention to him and she was right. She didn't know him.

So she could not love him.

No matter how many times she had said it on their wedding night, she didn't love him.

The realization hurt so much he stopped his thoughts. He wouldn't let himself go any further down that road. He knew better. He knew exactly what happened when a person let grief overwhelm him. He might have been in elementary school when his father left, but he had grieved. He had spent Christmas day on a chair by the window, watching it snow, waiting for his father to return, and when he didn't six-year-old Gerrick had fallen apart.

Then, when he was twelve his mother took him to spend his summer vacation with her sister, Gerrick's aunt, and simply never returned. She didn't give a word of explanation to him or his aunt. She just never came to pick him up. Only one day beyond her scheduled arrival, Gerrick knew what had happened and this time when he fell apart it wasn't the fear-based agony of a child, but the true grief of a boy on the brink of manhood. No one wanted him, and he knew it.

Anger and rebellion marked the next four years of his life, but on his sixteenth birthday everything changed. He suddenly realized the only person he could count on was himself, but he also saw that wasn't such a bad thing since he could control what he did. His life took a miraculous upturn. He got a job so he could begin to pay his own way. He made peace with his aunt and uncle and cautiously made friends at school. He didn't spend his life avoiding relationships, but he was careful and wise beyond his years.

Which was why he was amazed he had rolled the dice with Gina. He let his emotions overrule his common sense and now he was hurting almost as much as he had when he was twelve.

Except this time he had chosen his fate. This time he had a plan, but he hadn't followed it. When she proposed to him, he tossed his plan and his common sense out the window.

In some ways that made the hurt worse, because he knew this pain was his own fault.

He kept a tight hold on his control through the entire flight to Atlanta and on Sunday occupied himself with writing notes about his job for Josh Anderson, so he did not have time to think about Gina. He didn't want to be reminded of the things she'd said to him, their marriage or how stupid he had been to panic and marry her before she had a chance to catch up to his level of feelings. If he did, he knew he would crumble, or, worse, do something foolish.

On Monday morning he called Josh Anderson and Ethan McKenzie into Hilton Martin's office, which he had been using in Hilton's absence.

"Good morning, Josh, Ethan," Gerrick said with a nod to Ethan indicating he should close the office door. To look at him, no one would know the suffering of his soul. Gerrick held his emotions so tightly to his chest that even he didn't fully comprehend the extent of his pain.

"What's up?" Josh asked, taking a seat across the

desk from Gerrick. "I heard you went to Pennsylvania over the weekend. How was Hilton?"

"Weak but recovering," Gerrick said, as Ethan closed the door and took the second seat across the desk from Gerrick. "And because he's recovering so quickly and so well, we have some more important things to talk about. First of all, I never told anyone but…"

"But there's something between you and Gina," Ethan speculated, his dark eyes bright with merriment.

Josh grinned in agreement. "Olivia told me you got in to see Hilton the day of his heart attack, when none of us was allowed in because we're not in his immediate family. Olivia guessed…"

Gerrick held up his hands to stop Josh. "Don't guess. There's nothing happening between Gina and me. We went to Vegas that weekend to celebrate the fact that I had a new job.…"

"A new job?" Ethan said, sounding confused and reluctant.

Gerrick nodded. "This week is supposed to be the final week of my notice, but I'm going early. Today will be my last day. Hilton has known all along. He supported me during the interview process. He recommended me."

Josh swiped his hand across the back of his neck. "You can't be telling us you're leaving."

"That's exactly what I'm telling you," Gerrick said, rising from his seat to pace. He normally wasn't a fidgety person, but keeping such a tight rein on his emotions filled him with impulses and urges he almost couldn't control. But he did. He turned and smiled at the men in front of Hilton's desk. "One of you is going to have to take over."

"You're a more logical choice than I am," Ethan

said to Josh. "If only because you have to know more about the stores to promote them, but, frankly, Gerrick, I'm shocked that you're leaving. I'm shocked that you would leave us in a lurch when Hilton is so sick."

"My new job is as CEO of a grocery store chain in Maine. Their stock just went public. It's through the roof. The man who started the business is retiring, and everything is set up for this company to explode. I'm on the ground floor. A chance like this comes along once in a lifetime."

"And Hilton Martin has only really needed us once in a lifetime."

"Guys, he's been encouraging me to go."

Josh peered up. "And what does Gina say?"

Gerrick smiled at the irony. "She's emphatic that I go. She's also emphatic that you can handle this without me."

Ethan slapped his palm on the leather arm of his chair. "Then I guess you go," he said, but he didn't sound happy or encouraging.

"And we'll handle it," Josh said, as he rose.

The two men walked out of the office without another word and Gerrick rubbed his hands down his face. He had just lost two friends. First, he married Gina and thoroughly pushed her from his life. Then, to accommodate Gina, he had to leave Hilton-Cooper-Martin Foods, which alienated his friends. The only person he hadn't run off was Hilton and Gerrick suspected that if he ever found out about the secret Vegas wedding, Hilton wouldn't be his supporter anymore, either.

He remembered the old saw: be careful what you wish for because you may get it, and knew it was right. He had wished Gina would notice him, wished he could marry her before he moved to Maine, and both had happened.

And it had not only cost him any chance with her. It also cost his two best friends.

After settling her father in at the hospital in Atlanta, Gina arrived home the following Wednesday, exhausted but satisfied that her dad would eventually be back to normal. She joyfully paid the taxi driver and gave him a healthy tip because he lugged her assorted bags, boxes and mismatched suitcases into the foyer of the Martin mansion.

The first thing she saw after she turned away from the door was a note propped up against a vase on the small mahogany table beneath the large mirror. The envelope bore her name, so she reached for it and ripped it open.

She read it and tears unexpectedly filled her eyes. It said only,

I'm sorry,
Gerrick
P.S. By the way, I did love you. I might always love you.

Overcome, Gina dropped to sit on the bottom step of the stairway that spiraled to the second floor. The funny part of it was, she believed Gerrick really did love her. Or at least he loved the woman she had been in Vegas. Gina didn't know who that woman was but she did know she was gone for good. Particularly since she had more than a sneaking suspicion her father would begin to train her to take over the company once he returned to work, and her time would be taken up with facts, figures and negotiating strategies. So Gerrick was better off this way. The real Gina Martin wasn't the kind to fly to Vegas on the spur of the moment, to deliberately buy shimmering lace panties and bras because she knew the man shopping with her was attracted to her and she wanted to tease him.

The real Gina didn't tease people. The real Gina had thrown away the red bra and thong. The real Gina had invested the money she won playing blackjack.

Gerrick was much better off without her.

She pressed her lips together to stop their trembling, but couldn't stop the flood of tears that rolled down her cheeks. Though she didn't remember a big part of it— the most important part—that weekend in Vegas had been the best, most fun weekend of her entire life. But now she had to get back to her real world.

# Chapter Three

Between monitoring Josh's work as temporary head of Hilton-Cooper-Martin Foods and overseeing the treatment of her sick father, Gina initially didn't get much chance to think about Gerrick. When her thoughts did drift to him, she experienced the dull ache of missing him, but convinced herself that any thoughts she had of him were only the typical concern she would have for any co-worker who moved so far away. Particularly when weeks passed without so much as a phone call from him. The very fact that Gerrick never called—not even to check on her father—was proof any feelings he had for her were gone and any feelings she might have had for him were pointless.

At breakfast on the Monday of the fourth week after returning to Atlanta, Gina's father told her he was coming into the office and wanted her to call an employee meeting in the company cafeteria for ten o'clock that morning. She argued that he wasn't allowed to come in yet, though even she had to admit both his color and his energy were back. But he told her he had cleared this trip with his doctor and he was going in. Since he still had to get dressed, he told her to feel free to leave without him.

Gina drove to the corporate headquarters and she immediately wrote an e-mail instructing all department heads to have their employees in the cafeteria at ten. Assuming her father wanted everyone together to thank them for their cards, letters and phone calls, she had the maintenance department remove the tables from the room and arrange the chairs for theater seating, before they brought in the podium.

A good daughter and dutiful employee, at ten o'clock Gina was sitting on one of the folding chairs with her co-workers, when her father strode into the room and up to the podium. Wearing a navy-blue suit that complemented his very white hair and pale-blue eyes, Hilton Martin turned to face the assembled crowd. As the employees scrambled to their feet in thunderous applause, Gina also rose, clapping as loudly as everyone else. Her dad was the handsomest man on the face of the earth.

An image of Gerrick flashed in her mind contradicting that conclusion, but she shoved it aside. Not because Gerrick wasn't attractive, but because he was gone. That was done. She might occasionally think about him and wonder how he was doing, but if Ethan or Josh had gone to Maine, she would have wondered about them, too. She certainly didn't miss the man who had married her then never called her, and she didn't long to see him. No matter if that thought did pop into her brain, she wouldn't sanction it. He was gone. G-o-n-e.

"Sit. Sit," Hilton said, waving aside their applause, though Gina could see he was pleased by the welcome he received. "You're gonna make me feel like you missed me," he teased and the employees laughed. He motioned with his hand that everyone should sit and the applause stopped. The room grew quiet.

"Okay. I know you're wondering why I called you in this morning. Most of you are probably wondering why I'm even here."

"Yeah, this was my week to use your executive washroom," one of the employees called out, continuing the running joke the sales staff had about commandeering his washroom while he was recuperating.

"I'm having that place dusted for prints," Hilton said, giving back as good as he got. "And the cleaning crew for that room will be made up of everybody whose prints I find."

That brought another spurt of laughter, followed by another round of applause and Gina breathed a long sigh of relief. Her father looked a little tired, but he was essentially back to normal. At least as normal as he could be until he had his bypass surgery. In fact, she suspected his upcoming surgery was the reason he had returned prematurely. He probably wanted to clear up everything he could before he had to take off another long span of recovery time. Specifically, he had to officially appoint Josh as head of Operations and give him temporary power to run the company.

"Anyway, you're here for two reasons. First, I want to thank you for the cards, flowers, gifts, fruit baskets, homemade cookies and phone calls." His eyes misted and his throat sounded tight. "Thank you."

The employees again applauded exuberantly, and Hilton took the opportunity to compose himself. When the commotion died down, he said, "The second reason I brought you here is to tell you that I have decided to retire."

''What?''

Gina wasn't the only person who had said that out loud. Beside her, Ethan McKenzie and Josh Anderson both said the same thing. It wasn't unusual for her fun-loving father to dramatically make surprise announcements that even upper-echelon staff didn't know about. But this wasn't a surprise. It was a disaster. She, Ethan and Josh knew they weren't ready to take over. They might have done well in the short-term, but they couldn't run the company indefinitely.

''Now, hear me out. I didn't mention to anyone that I was thinking about retiring,'' he said, glancing apologetically at Gina, Josh and Ethan, ''because I wanted to be sure the person I picked to replace me could take the job before I announced I was leaving. And I got a phone call early this morning indicating my replacement would be here today so I decided there was no reason to wait to make the transition.''

Everyone in the room appeared dumbfounded. Gina simply stared at her father realizing she, Ethan and Josh didn't have to take over. Actually, the change wouldn't affect Ethan and Josh at all. Ethan already headed his department and Josh had had no choice but to assume the leadership position in Operations when Gerrick left. Both of them were in place. But for Gina, her father's leaving the company was staggering. It meant it would not be her dad who trained her to run the business. A stranger would show her the ropes, and she wasn't sure how she felt about that.

''Having a heart attack is a really frightening thing,'' her father continued. ''But more than being frightening, it was an eye opener.'' He leaned down on the podium, getting comfortable, making everyone feel he believed he was talking to his closest friends. Gina knew that was because he was. He considered every person he employed a friend of sorts and he would have no compunction about confiding in them.

"I want to travel. I want to play golf. I actually want to try to find somebody to share my life with."

"You're getting married?" somebody from the audience yelled.

"I hope to get that lucky, but I haven't even had a girlfriend in six years. I haven't had a date in two." He paused and shook his head. "People, my personal life sucks."

That comment brought another burst of laughter followed by a long round of applause.

"Anyway," Hilton said when they had quieted down. "I suppose what I'm saying is that I want a life. Frankly, I can afford to have one, so I'm going to."

"You go, Hilt-eeee."

Gina's father chuckled. "Okay, then you approve?"

The employees again began to applaud. In a show of support, Ethan McKenzie rose. So did Josh. So did Gina. Her father was sick, needed surgery, wanted a life. How could she not support him? If she had to be trained by a stranger, then so be it.

Soon every person in the room was on his or her feet. The duration and volume of the applause was amazing. After several minutes, Hilton finally insisted they stop. Reluctantly, the applause dwindled to a halt. Everyone sat again.

"Okay, while I've got you sympathetic, I'm also going to remind you that I'm getting bypass surgery in eight weeks. So my replacement can't afford to fail. I need to know you will be as good to him as you've been to me."

Again, every employee rose to his or her feet. Again,

the applause lasted so long Hilton had to insist they stop.

"So my guy is going to get your cooperation?"

After shouts and calls of support, Hilton added, "That's good because it's Gerrick Green."

Again, her father's news resulted in resounding silence. Gina sat frozen as contradictory reactions bounced through her. Just hearing Gerrick's name made her breath catch and her muscles quiver, but her stomach also plummeted. If Gerrick was the new CEO, he would be the person to train her. She could be in his company every hour of every day for *years,* once she came under his tutelage.

"In fact, Gerrick is waiting in my office. I'll be leaving at one. He'll be taking over today."

Gina's chest tightened from the shock of that. Someone in the audience shouted, "But he quit. He left in the middle of a crisis."

"No one here knows the real story behind why Gerrick didn't stay," Gina's father said neutrally, though he glanced at Gina, and her chest tightened another notch. It was bad enough to realize she was about to come face-to-face with Gerrick, but now she had to wonder how he had explained his disappearance to her father.

He couldn't have...

He wouldn't have...

"Six months before my heart attack, Gerrick began interviewing for the position he left Hilton-Cooper-Martin Foods to take. It was a long, difficult process. He had to win over a skeptical board of directors for a company that had been around for a decade, but hadn't gone public with its stock until the year before. He aced those interviews. He was the man they wanted."

"So why doesn't he stay there?"

"Because he *is* loyal to us. When I called and told him I was retiring, and that he was my choice for replacement, he didn't hesitate. He said he would find a way out of his contract, then helped his new company locate someone to fill his position."

From that explanation Gina believed that Gerrick hadn't told her father anything about their marriage, and she relaxed, but she also mentally calculated in her head that her father had asked Gerrick to return the week after his catheterization...probably mere days after Gerrick had left. She didn't even know her dad knew Gerrick had gone. Worse, when she considered that Gerrick had made the decision to come back less than a week after he wrote a note saying he might always love her, she had to wonder about Gerrick's motives in returning. What if he had returned for her?

*Oh, God! He had every right in the world to return for her. They had never divorced! She was still married to him!*

"I'm not going to ask twice for your cooperation with Gerrick. I'm going to assume I have it. Not just because I need it, but because I know I can count on you. You're the best employees in Atlanta."

That got another round of applause. Gina's co-workers again rose to their feet. Hilton apparently considered that the approval he sought and didn't wait for further agreement, but walked away from the podium and directly to Gina, Ethan and Josh.

"He's in my office. I want the three of you there immediately to get rid of any bad blood and make him feel welcome. In fact, walk with me."

Josh and Ethan nodded.

Still too confused to face Gerrick yet, Gina said, "I need to stop in my office."

"What for?"

*Several deep breaths. A minute to figure out what to do. Maybe the chance to look for an escape route?*

"I... It's... Don't worry about it, okay?"

"Oh, it's a woman's thing," Hilton said knowingly, but he also didn't argue. "We'll see you in my office. But don't be longer than ten minutes."

Gina nodded, glad her father labeled everything he didn't understand a "woman's thing" because now she had some time to try to figure out what to do. Dodging anybody who might potentially stop her to talk, Gina raced down the hall, through her secretary's station and into her office. She shut the door, and for good measure went into her private washroom.

She also closed that door.

She was so shocked, she couldn't even scream. Instead, she stood with her hands braced on the black porcelain sink taking deep breaths. Then she lifted her face and stared at her reflection in the mirror.

Her bright-pink top reflected the happy, springlike mood of the warm and sunny late March weather with which Atlanta had been blessed, so did her flowered skirt. Unfortunately, that meant she wasn't wearing a jacket and didn't look like a business associate. She looked like a person...

No, darn it! She looked like a *girl*. Actually, with her cheeks flushed, she looked like an excited bride, eager to see her new husband.

"Great," Gina mumbled then dropped her head for a few more deep breaths and another few minutes to remind herself that the husband she was so eager to see had not called her, not once, since he left, and that her marriage was a mistake. Unfortunately, when she brought her head back up the same excited woman stared back at her.

At least her hair was good, Gina thought. Cut to just above her shoulders, it curved under nicely this morning. She combed her fingers through the fat tresses at her nape and fluffed them out a little, recognizing that the warmth of the sable color definitely complemented her face, which, luckily, had cooperated by retaining the light coat of foundation and lipstick she had applied. When Gerrick saw her, she knew he wouldn't turn and run.

Realizing where her thoughts had gone, Gina cupped her head in her hands. What was she doing? She was supposed to be figuring out how she would deal with seeing him again. Not checking her makeup and fluffing her hair!

What was it about him that turned her into somebody she didn't even recognize?

With her time running out, Gina decided she would have to sort through her contradictory personal reactions later. Right now she had to go to this meeting, because, like it or not, she had to work with him. Technically, the paths of the CEO and the Human Resources director hardly crossed—unless, or until, he began to train her. But by then she should be completely under control. She was too logical to moon over someone who hadn't called her—someone who didn't love her—no matter what that darned note said. Plus, she was the one who had called a halt to their marriage. And she had had good reasons. She couldn't actually remember them right now, but she did know she had plenty of them. She wasn't negating a sound decision just because of a stomachful of butterflies and a bunch of emotions that made no sense.

Satisfied with that conclusion, she strode out of her bathroom, then exited her office only to find her father sitting on the corner of her secretary's desk, waiting for her.

"Dad?"

"Hey."

She shook her head as if confused. "What's up? I thought we were meeting in your office?"

"I just wanted to make sure you were okay."

"I'm fine," she said, though her voice quivered because something was wrong. Her father never checked on her. Especially not when he thought she was handling a "woman's thing." More than that, though, when it came to her job, he expected her to be tough. Sure. Secure. That was why he hadn't apprised her of Gerrick's return any more than he had told Josh or Ethan. He treated her the same way he treated any other employee. She didn't get special consideration. No heads-up. No warnings.

Something was definitely wrong.

He sighed. "All right. I think we need to get some cards out on the table about you and Gerrick."

Gina's heart stopped and her muscles tingled with dread. She combined that comment with the look her father had given her in the cafeteria when he said no one fully understood Gerrick's reasons for leaving, and it suddenly struck her that he could very well know about her ill-fated marriage. Her dad had more sources for information than any person had a right to have, and it wasn't such a stretch to think he had discovered she'd flitted off to Vegas, gotten swept away in the noise, lights and champagne, married his favorite vice president and then dumped him. Oh, God, she had dumped her father's favorite vice president!

She fought the urge to squeeze her eyes shut. She was a dead woman!

"I know what happened between you and Gerrick. I was going to pretend I didn't and just bring him back and force you to deal with it, but I changed my mind."

"Dad, I…"

He held up his hand so she would let him have his say. "I'm not going to criticize.…"

Though her skin had grown cold and clammy, and Gina was sure she might faint because her breathing was shallow—and her stomach was still back in the cafeteria—she managed to stay on her feet and even smile slightly.

"…but you shouldn't have fired him."

"What?"

"Well, maybe fired is too strong of a word."

Aghast, Gina said, "I didn't fire him."

"You asked him to leave."

"I didn't…" Actually, she had. Now that she thought about it, insisting that he take his new job could be construed as asking him to leave. "But it wasn't like it sounds. I didn't want him to lose his opportunity. Between Josh and Ethan, I knew the company would get by."

"And you were right. I'm also assuming that you didn't intend to make Gerrick feel that leaving was his only alternative." He rose and laid his arm across her shoulders and instinctively Gina shifted her head to protect her perfect hair.

She almost groaned. She wasn't supposed to care how she looked! She was supposed to be out of love with Gerrick…if she had ever *been* in love with Gerrick. Plus, he wasn't in love with her. He couldn't be or he would have called. Worse yet, her father was now involved, or at least watching. He may not know everything but he knew something. And right now she didn't have a clue what that was.

"I didn't intend to make him feel fired."

"I think you forget that as Human Resources director anything you say is taken in the context of your position. When you tell someone to go, you are firing him."

"I didn't fire him," Gina mumbled.

"Well, he didn't say that you did, but he said you wouldn't let him stay. You put him between a rock and a hard place."

"He's such a whiner."

Though she hadn't meant to make the comment out loud, Gina was glad she had because her father laughed.

"He is not a whiner. I badgered him into explaining why he left. I badgered him into coming back. That was when he explained why he felt he couldn't come back."

"How does he do that?"

"Do what?"

"Come out of everything looking innocent."

"Maybe because he is innocent. He's a good guy, trying to work to his potential by taking the best job available to him." He paused, caught Gina's gaze. "Unless there's something about this situation I don't know."

Not about to go into that minefield for all the tea in China, particularly not after remembering that Gerrick was her dad's favorite, Gina shook her head.

"Okay, then, here's the deal. If the people in this company give him a hard time for leaving when I was sick, you're actually the one responsible."

Gina gasped in surprise, then clamped her mouth

shut. Without the knowledge of her marriage, her father was right.

"So you have to be his white knight."

*Oh, geez!*

"What exactly does a white knight do in this case?"

"You have to clear the path. Support everything he says and does. Any time you hear a rumor that someone isn't happy with him, you need to call that person into your office and enthusiastically state that you're behind Gerrick one hundred percent."

"Okay," she said humbly, because, really, this didn't sound too bad.

"And I want you to eat lunch with him in the cafeteria every day so the employees see every day that you support him."

"Dad! I don't eat lunch every day!"

"Well, now you're going to start," he said firmly and Gina knew he wasn't taking no for an answer. He genuinely believed she had inadvertently fired Gerrick, and in a sense he was right. But more than that, as long as he believed the strain that was undoubtedly going to exist between her and Gerrick was because she had fired him, it actually made her life a little easier.

"I'm going to get fat," she mumbled, heading for the door.

"You can afford to gain ten pounds. If you gain more, I have the number for an excellent spa."

"Yeah, right," Gina said. If she ever saw champagne or a slot machine again, she would run in the other direction. Or at least as far away from Gerrick as she could get. She had no idea how he had done it but somehow or another he had managed to turn this whole situation to his favor. Twenty minutes ago anybody in this building would have boldly proclaimed he was an inconsiderate lout who left Hilton-Cooper-Martin high and dry and didn't care enough about her father to even call to see how he was doing. Now, suddenly, he was as sainted as Mother Teresa. And in looking good he also managed to make her look bad.

Gina and her father walked to his office in complete silence. Both said hello to his secretary as they passed her workstation. Then, announcing their arrival as they stepped into his huge, ornate office, Hilton said, "Here we are."

Gina didn't look at the big cherry-wood desk, the bookcases filled with tattered volumes of the classics or the wall of windows at the back of the room, letting in bright beams of late-morning sunlight. Her eyes scanned until they homed in on her nemesis, Gerrick Green.

Simultaneously, his eyes found hers. Their gazes locked. Hers hardened. His remained neutral.

Her father took her elbow and led her to a round table laden with the employee gifts of cookies, candies, crackers and cheeses because that was where Josh, Ethan and Gerrick had gathered. But when her father handed her a glass of champagne, she recoiled as if it had bitten her.

"I don't think so."

"Come on," Hilton chided teasingly. "I think a toast is in order."

Not about to call more attention to herself by arguing, Gina reluctantly took the glass from her father's hand.

"Okay, then," Hilton said, raising his drink. "A toast to my enjoying the rest of my life and to you four. May running this company bring you as much joy and success as it's brought me."

"Hear! Hear!"

Hilton shook his head. "I'm not done. I want to toast my retirement, and you guys enjoying your time running the company, but I need to add that I hope none of you will be like me and stay so long or work so hard that you miss the good things in life. I hope all four of you will recognize when it's time to leave, and go."

Though everyone raised his or her glass, Gerrick laughed. "I tried to leave and you wouldn't let me."

"It wasn't your time," Hilton said simply and changed the subject to begin redistributing the workload. Because Josh had basically run the company in Hilton's absence, Gina's father officially promoted him into Gerrick's old position as head of Operations and made both Josh and Ethan vice presidents.

The men chuckled and slapped each other on the back as they drank their champagne and began to toast each other's success. But though Gina participated in all the toasts, she barely sipped her champagne. No way in hell was she going to be in the same room with Gerrick and an open bottle of liquor again. Since she was, she would be extremely careful.

Her father had lunch brought up from the cafeteria, and it arrived a few minutes after eleven. Though this was supposed to be a party of sorts, when they sat down to eat it continued to be a business meeting as her father outlined his expectations of his new CEO and vice presidents, with Gerrick also voicing his ideas.

Finishing her tuna melt, Gina grudgingly admitted that Gerrick was the right person to take over for her father, and Hilton could retire in peace. Gerrick knew everything about the company and was a well-rounded businessperson, but that didn't mean she should be married to him.

For the next several years he would be training her

to do the mammoth job of running this company. It would be better if they didn't have a personal relationship while he did it.

"Well, I'm leaving," Hilton said, rising, but he snapped his fingers as if he forgot something. "I can't. I have to meet with the union before I go."

"Good, I'll…" Gerrick began.

But Hilton interrupted him. "No. No. This is private. More personal than business. We won't need you. Besides, I want you and Gina to meet right now in her office and smooth any ruffled feathers. Exactly one hour from now when I leave," he said, glancing at his watch. "I want to see the two of you kiss and make up."

Gerrick laughed at her father's joke, but Gina's eyes narrowed, as she studied her overconfident, overcasual dad. He knew she and Gerrick had married. Damn it! She knew he knew! But she just couldn't figure out why he wouldn't admit it or what he planned to accomplish by not confronting them.

After a quick round of goodbyes, Gina and Gerrick walked to her office. Neither said a word. At first, Gina thought she should try to make polite small talk, but the longer they walked without speaking, the more it felt like a competition, as if the loser would be the one who spoke first.

By the time they strode past her secretary and through her office door, Gina was proud of herself for not uttering one sound. Gerrick greeted her secretary, then followed Gina into her office.

Given that he had complained to her father that she had told him to leave, she expected him to jump her the minute he closed the door. But when she rounded her desk to face him, he was smiling, not neutral as he had been in her father's office, and she froze, caught by an unexpected need to simply drink in the sight of him. His shiny black hair complemented his perfectly tailored black suit, which made him look tall and broad-shouldered. His green eyes always seemed to sparkle with warmth. Worse, she was getting those pangs of missing him again.

This was trouble.

Especially since he wasn't angry with her. In fact, he looked downright glad to see her. The last private words she had from him were in a note that told her he would always love her. And though she wasn't entirely sure why and in spite of trying to talk herself out of it, she had missed him.

And, he had already successfully seduced her once. This time not only were they alone behind closed doors, but also they were married.

"Gina, I'm sorry."

His tone of voice didn't match the expression on his face and Gina frowned. She wouldn't have been surprised if he had yelled at her. She wouldn't have been shocked if he had grabbed her shoulders and kissed her. But an apology was the last thing she expected.

Her frown deepened. "What?"

"I'm sorry. Your dad misconstrued everything I told him about my leaving."

"He's the one who came up with the firing scenario?"

"Yes. I never would have told him that you asked me to leave if he hadn't hounded me. I'm not a whiner."

"Right." Gina sat on the tall-backed black leather chair behind her desk, and motioned for him to take the seat across from her, putting a sturdy piece of furniture between them on the off chance that this apology was just a way to get her guard down. "If that's the case, then I don't think we need to go any further. All is forgiven. And we have nothing to talk about."

Gerrick caught her gaze. This time he wasn't smiling. His eyes were warm, but serious. "Actually, we have plenty to talk about."

Gina drew a long breath, not able to read him or figure out what he felt they should discuss. She had already told him their marriage was a mistake, and he had given tacit agreement by not calling to talk her out of that opinion. Unless, he hadn't called because he knew he was coming back in a few weeks and decided to have the conversation face-to-face...

Oh, God he might be here to seduce her after all!

Mercifully, the phone rang. She grabbed it. "Hello?"

"I'm sorry to bother you, Gina, but Mr. Green has a call."

"Okay," Gina said, glad for a few minutes to reassemble her arguments against their relationship. "He'll take it in here."

She handed the phone to Gerrick. "You have a call. Just say hello. Once Marci hangs up your call will be there."

Gerrick smiled and shook his head. "Gina, I've been gone five or six weeks. I haven't forgotten how to operate the phones."

"Yeah. Right. Sorry," Gina said.

Gerrick said, "Hello," then paused before gasping, "Janice!" As he said the name, he caught Gina's gaze and immediately turned away from her. He didn't exactly shield her from hearing his end of the conversation, but he had definitely made it so that she couldn't see his face. "I hadn't expected to hear from you!"

*Hah! A girlfriend!* No wonder he turned away. Not

even divorced, simply apart for a few weeks, and already he had someone else.

She settled back in her chair. No need to think this through. No need to try and come up with arguments for a divorce. He had just handed her the perfect out. Adultery.

Boy, he was making this easy.

She tugged the hem of her shirt over her flowered skirt, pretending to be totally disinterested.

"I'm sorry I didn't call you before I left. Everything just happened so fast."

Gina struggled to contain a smirk. This was perfect.

"I know that it seems like I left you high and dry. But on the plane coming down here I thought of someone to replace me."

She frowned. He had found a person to replace him at the job he had just left. Now he had a replacement for himself as a boyfriend. She wondered if he had a recommendation for a replacement husband.

"Alice Monroe who worked with me for the few weeks I was at General Groceries is perfect for the job. She's their event coordinator. If you think about it there are tons of similarities to that job and planning a fundraiser."

Gina's frown deepened.

"That fire was a tragedy. Every time I close my eyes, I see the face of that little boy holding the teddy bear and crying, and I almost can't handle it. Somebody's got to help those people. I'm glad your foundation stepped in to manage the donations, and I know Mr. Evans at General Groceries will volunteer Alice Monroe's time to take my place as chairman of the fundraiser."

Gina slid down in her chair.

"I'll be back in Maine the week of the event. And, of course, they'll get my check."

Gina sighed. Okay. So he wasn't a two-timer and he wasn't a whiner. But that didn't mean she should be married to him.

"I have an enormous soft spot where kids are concerned."

Damn it! Did the man have to be such a nice guy?

Still talking on her phone, he rose and removed his jacket. Gina couldn't help but notice how trim and sexy his body was. She pulled her eyes away and looked at the ceiling, trying not to remember that she had slept with this man, made passionate love with this man. Unfortunately, the thought slipped through. Worse, so did regret. Not regret that she had slept with him, but regret that she didn't remember sleeping with him.

Okay. That made her rise to pace. Gerrick paced on one side of her desk. She paced on the other. Seeing the ridiculousness of that, she stopped and stared out the big window.

"I've got a lot of personal things to do here before I can get back in touch. Mostly I want to find a house. Make a home. I've never really had one and now that I'm older, I've decided to do that for myself."

Gina swallowed. She heard the restless loneliness in his voice and recognized it. She had felt the same way almost every day of the year after Chad had broken their engagement. In fact, she blamed it on Chad, though eventually she understood that never having moved from her childhood home was the real culprit. Not having her own identity was starting to be awkward. Like Gerrick, she thought that getting her own house would cure the emptiness, but she later realized it would only solve part of the problem. Because she didn't want a house. She wanted a home. Her own home.

And so did he. If she looked at this the right way, they were something like kindred spirits. He was a handsome, nice guy searching for a home. She was a reasonably attractive, sensitive woman searching for a home, a place, an identity. And that was why they had clicked so quickly in Vegas. They were both lonely. They wanted more out of life than what they had. And they were incredibly attracted to each other.

The problem wasn't that they had gotten married, the problem was that they had married too quickly. Now that she wasn't under the weight of worry about her father, it was all very clear.

"Sorry about that," Gerrick said when he hung up her phone.

"That's okay," she said, smiling ruefully. She had no idea what they were supposed to do, but she did finally see that getting married had not been a bad idea. Just a premature one. And maybe he wasn't wrong to want to reopen discussions on their relationship.

"So, we have a few things we need to iron out."

Gina nodded. "Yes, we do." She tapped a pencil on her desk. She wasn't ready to be married, but since her father appeared to already know about their marriage they couldn't just separate. She supposed that what they needed to do was date, but she had no idea how to start that discussion.

She stalled. "So how did you get roped into chairing a fund-raiser less than a week after you arrived?"

"Big fire. An apartment building. The people are in the segment of the population that falls through the cracks. Most have minimum-wage jobs. Lots are single mothers. The landlord wasn't going to rebuild."

Gina sat back on her chair, put her elbow on the leather arm and rested her chin in the L created by her thumb and forefinger. "What were you going to do?"

"The fund-raiser was actually a double duty dinner. Ostensibly, we were getting people together to raise money to help the families, but while we had the most wealthy citizens of the area in one room, I was going to try to form a group of investors to build another apartment building."

She glanced up. "You were?"

"I can't afford to do it myself, but if I got enough people to kick in, I figured we could do it."

"It doesn't sound like you would make much profit."

"Not everything you do in life is supposed to be for profit."

Gina smiled. "No, I guess not." Every word he said, everything she discovered about him only made her realize what a perfect husband he would make. With her guard down because of alcohol, the decision to marry him must have looked like a no-brainer. She shook her head. "Whatever you're asking as an investment, count me in."

He grinned at her. "Bottom of the scale or top of the scale?"

"How high is the top?"

"Low six figures."

She whistled.

"You can invest whatever you want."

She shook her head again. "No, you're right. Not everything in life is supposed to be for profit. I've always had everything I needed, and sometimes I don't appreciate it. Put me at the top of the scale."

He gaped at her. "Really?"

She nodded. "Really."

"If I didn't think it would stir up a nest of trouble, I would hug you."

"Yeah, well, that's the other thing we need to talk about." She felt completely different now than she had in that hospital in Pennsylvania. She was glad enough time had passed for her to settle down emotionally, and she was glad her father had brought Gerrick home. She was also glad Gerrick had gotten that phone call, because their being together made perfect sense to her now.

"I know," he said then cleared his throat. "You want a divorce."

"Actually, I'm not sure that's the right thing to do."

He stared at her. "You have to be kidding! Gina, we made a big mistake in Vegas. Even if you don't want out, I do."

# Chapter Four

Gerrick shoved his key card into his hotel door lock and when the light turned green, pushed his way into his room. Tired, confused, he dropped his briefcase on the mauve-and-pink floral-print bedspread that matched the curtains, then fell into one of the captain's chairs by the round table near the window and scrubbed his hands down his face.

The last five minutes he spent in Gina's office were the hardest of his life. But he had made it through without saying anything he would regret and without falling at her feet and admitting that he didn't want a divorce, either. Though he thought he should be proud of himself, he felt frustration and anger.

The stricken look on her face was enough to make any man drop everything, even his pride, and agree with anything she said, but Gerrick knew he couldn't. The weeks in Maine had been very positive, very conducive to clearing his head, and he was on his way to being over her and their ill-fated marriage. He wouldn't reopen those old wounds.

But, oh, he had been tempted.

The minute he had laid eyes on her that morning, he had wanted to haul her into his arms and kiss her senseless. He remembered every second of their twenty-four hours together as man and wife. He remembered making love to her in vivid detail. But he also reminded himself that she had no memory of the most important day of his life. Not only did he believe she wasn't committed to the relationship—particularly since she only suggested she "might" want to "try" something to see if they could make this marriage work—but also she had hurt him. He would be a fool to risk his heart a second time.

He refused to think about how lonely he was, or the fact that he'd grown so accustomed to being on his own that he hadn't realized his life was empty until he began to pursue Gina. As they got closer, he naturally slipped into planning their future together and now there was a void without that vision. Even now, if he closed his eyes he could still see it. He could still see a future filled with possibilities for them.

He was such an idiot. He knew better than to create outlandish plans or dream dreams involving someone unreliable. His parents had taught him that. He wasn't a man who only rolled the dice on sure things, but he was a man who knew the truth when it was staring him in the face and the truth was Gina Martin didn't love him. He couldn't pretend that she did. She might want to give their marriage a try, but he couldn't risk the pain if he opened himself up to her again, and they dated or whatever she had in mind, and then she decided she didn't want him.

To assure his mental health and stability, not to mention the stability of his employment situation, he had told her this afternoon that he didn't want to waste her time or his on something that probably wouldn't work, and that he wanted to file for divorce that week. *He* would file. *He* would pay expenses. He just wanted out.

That was when her face became stricken and that was when he almost buckled under. But he didn't. He had stood up from the chair in front of her desk and left her office.

So instead of having dinner with the woman he adored, he was here in this lifeless hotel room, about to order room service...again. It hadn't bothered him to be alone for the past ten years and it angered him that it bothered him now. But he wouldn't blame Gina and he wouldn't blame himself. He would deal with it.

At eleven-thirty the next day, Gina walked up to Gerrick's office doorway. Because he was busily writing in his day planner, she could have turned and run but she didn't. In spite of the way he rejected her the afternoon before, she had to keep her promise to her father to eat lunch with Gerrick every day. Plus, she knew Gerrick was right. Though their last meeting had ended embarrassingly, and left her with a dull ache of remorse over what might have been, she agreed they shouldn't stay married simply because they had gotten married. Just as he said, they had to get on with their lives as if that trip hadn't happened. Unfortunately, she also couldn't help but think that was a very odd sentiment from a man who had written her a note saying he loved her and might always love her.

Wishing she could forget that darned note, she suppressed a disappointed sigh and continued watching

Gerrick, waiting for him to be finished writing. With his dark hair and pale eyes, he looked fabulous in his navy-blue suit, white shirt and emerald-green print tie. But more than that, he exuded confidence and capability, as if he were always destined for the seat of power. He was gorgeous, nice *and* smart.

She held back another sigh. Was it any wonder that when the opportunity presented itself she had snagged it and married him?

Turning a page in the date book, he glanced up and saw her. His eyebrows rose in surprise and he said, "Yes?"

"My father said we have to eat lunch together every day as my way of showing the employees that I support you."

"That's not necessary..."

"Don't argue, Gerrick. I don't know how my dad finds out everything that happens, but he does, and if I don't do something I promised, he's going to be furious. He's too sick to annoy right now."

"Okay," Gerrick said, and closed his calendar, apparently agreeing that her father had some kind of spy who fed him inside information and also that Hilton Martin was too sick to aggravate. "I'm ready if you're ready."

This time she didn't stop her sigh. She let it out on a long, disgusted breath. "I'm as ready as I'll ever be."

Gerrick laughed and stepped away from his desk. "Eating with me isn't a death sentence."

"No. But after our discussion yesterday, I think we said everything we needed to say to each other." She turned and led the way out of his office. "It's going to be a long hour if we have nothing to talk about."

"Well, put your mind at ease," Gerrick said, as they

passed Hilton's secretary, Joanna, a tall redhead who had agreed to be Gerrick's secretary. "Because as a CEO speaking to the director of Human Resources, I have plenty of things to talk about with you."

"Really?" she asked pleasantly surprised.

"Sure. Human Resources is an important function."

"Oh, we're fluff," Gina said, dismissing his praise with a wave of her hand. "I mean, I know the worker's compensation things I do are important. Benefits are important. Hiring and firing is important. But we're an expense. We don't actually make money. As far as the business is concerned, if we fell upon hard times, all my tasks could be reassigned and my department and I could be the first to go."

"I'll have to remember that."

"The only way you can get rid of my department is if *you* push the company into hard times. And I wouldn't advise it."

"And I really don't agree with your assessment of your department's place in the company. Especially, when I have some reorganization I want to do and for which I'll need your help."

"Really?" Gina asked, again pleasantly surprised as she stepped into the cafeteria. Unlike the theater seating of the day before for her father's meeting, the room had been rearranged and tables stood in neat rows with chairs lining both sides. The lunch line was open.

She reached for an apple. "How can I help?"

Gerrick took a tuna sandwich and a salad. "I want to talk about the structure of our departments and the reasons they're set up the way they are. Then, I need to see some personnel files. Before you give them to me, I would like you to give me quick verbal summaries of everything you know about each of my candidates so I don't have to read entire files, and so I can have your insights.''

"Are you going to promote or fire these people?"

"Neither. I'm shifting them around."

Because most employees ate at twelve, the cafeteria line was short. They reached the cash register quickly and before she could stop him, Gerrick paid for her lunch.

She sighed. "You can't do things like that."

"Why not?"

"Because it's going to get expensive if my dad insists we eat together until he's satisfied the staff accepts you. You could be buying my lunch for the rest of the year."

He leaned close and whispered in her ear. "That's okay. I can handle it. I got a raise."

Shivers of awareness vibrated through her at his nearness and the tickle of his words against her ear. She shook her head as if annoyed, but really to mask her pleasure at being close to him. He always smelled great, looked great and was fun to be around. Even as a CEO he couldn't behave completely. The man simply loved to tease.

"I saw your raise."

"Then you know it's going to suck up all your family's shareholder dividends for this quarter. If you've got a Lexus on layaway, I'd tell the dealer to put it back if I were you."

Gina couldn't help it. She laughed. "Just pick a table."

He chose a spot in the center of things and Gina gingerly set down her tray. "People are going to be able to hear us talking."

"I thought that was the whole point."

"No, people are supposed to *see* us getting along and

working together, not necessarily hear what we're saying."

"Well, look at it this way, then. No one will think we're planning covert strategies if they can hear our conversation. Besides, we won't use names when we talk. We'll only discuss the department structures and the new positions I want to create."

"Don't you have something else we could discuss besides things that directly affect employees?" Gina asked, uncomfortable with talking about potential changes out in the open.

He set his napkin on his lap. "I'm redecorating my office, but that doesn't really concern you."

His observation indicated he intended to limit the discussion to human resource related topics. Gina was stung, but she knew she didn't have the right to be upset. She drew them back into the conversation about the structure of the departments. Though Gerrick outlined his plan casually it was clear he didn't intend to move a few people. What he described would be a full-scale reorganization.

They discussed his ideas for an entire hour, but Gina still didn't think that he had enough information to start considering employee shifts. She asked him for the time to put together specific data from employee files and he agreed to meet with her again in his office after four.

Gina nodded her consent, then she picked up her tray and left him because it was clear he was going to schmooze. Though no one had bothered him while Gina was at his table, the second Gina stood, other employees scooted over to congratulate him and before she had tossed the contents of her tray into the trash, he was on a roll. Making jokes. Laughing. Accepting congratulations and even a few apologies from people who admitted they had accused him of jumping ship. He brushed everybody's concern aside, and rather than have anybody feel guilty or ill at ease, he made another joke.

The laughter that followed her out the door sort of bugged her. He was so casual, so comfortable, with the other employees that he made her feel awkward. It wasn't that he wasn't nice and polite with her. He was. He even teased her. But there was something missing. He wasn't as friendly with her as he was with the others. And nowhere near the same as he had been before their disastrous trip to Vegas. And that was the bottom line. It almost seemed that by marrying him she had ruined their friendship.

As she and her secretary pulled files, Gina realized that was why his coolness annoyed her and that maybe she did have a reason to be upset with him and his insulting aloofness. For Pete's sake they had been friends enough to get married! And it wasn't like she had asked *him* to marry *her*. It was undoubtedly a mutual decision. Plus, she wasn't the one who had written the note about loving him and probably always loving him…

And what was the deal with that anyway? Shouldn't that note count for something as far as their trying to make their marriage work? How could he just blurt that he had no intention of trying? She hadn't thought that he would leap at the chance to get back together, but she had believed that a man who claimed to love her and who lamented that he might always love her would at least want to consider the possibility of reconciliation.

But no. He didn't even want to consider it. He hadn't stumbled and fumbled over his refusal the day before.

He had been quite clear. He just wanted out. Their relationship was over.

*Well, great. Fine. Whatever,* she thought, dragging an armload of files into her office. So what if it was over? Lord knew it wasn't like she was pining for a man who had been hers for years. They had had a personal relationship exactly twenty-four hours before they rushed to the altar. She would get over this. Years from now, she would probably look back on it and laugh.

Reviewing files and making notes, she remembered the shock of waking up married and how nervous she had been and—darn it—she did laugh. She had missed the humor of the situation as it was happening, but with a few weeks of buffer time to tone down her embarrassment, she had to admit it was funny. Having the red bra on the lamp and the red thong looped from a curtain was hysterical. In fact, she burst into giggles. And Gerrick hadn't said a word. Nope. All what he'd done was kiss her.

She sighed.

He was a fabulous kisser. No, *they* were a pretty good kissing team. When she had finally talked herself into keeping the marriage in spite of not remembering the wedding, she had kissed him back and it was explosive. She got chills now, just thinking about it.

Their return flight from Vegas, though, was even better. She dreamily remembered how romantic he was, and rested her chin on her closed fist with another wistful sigh. In her mind's eye she saw every single minute of their flight, heard every comment, considered every shared glance and sighed about every darned time he had kissed her hand. It was very hard to reconcile the man on that plane with the man who currently inhabited her father's office.

And *that* was the problem. She felt like she was dealing with two different men. One loved her, one didn't. And she wished the one who loved her would come back.

Before Gina knew it, it was four o'clock. Though she wasn't completely finished with her review, she scooped up her files and her notes and scrambled to Gerrick's office. His secretary wasn't at her desk and his door was open, so she simply barreled through Joanna's workstation. She stopped abruptly when she saw he was seated at the small conference table in the corner of the room, explaining something to a dreamy-eyed Lawanna Johnson, head of the Perishable Distribution Center.

Gina didn't have to wonder why Lawanna was dreamy eyed. Even without a jacket and with his tie loose, Gerrick was gorgeous. With those green eyes, he could reduce most women to a fainting swoon. But this afternoon with the sleeves of his white shirt rolled to his elbows, his hair a mite ruffled and his expression serious and concerned, no woman stood a chance.

He leaned in, counseling Lawanna with a sincerity that demonstrated he was a genuinely nice person, and Gina suddenly realized he was back. *This* was the man she remembered. The guy she had expected to see yesterday and at lunch today. The guy so sincere it was impossible not to trust him and so handsome he took her breath away.

Her arms laden with files, Gina stood in his doorway and stared dreamily. To think, she was married to him.

As if Lawanna had done something to alert Gerrick to Gina's presence, he suddenly turned to face the door. "Can I help you, Gina?"

"We were supposed to meet at four."

"Oh, that's right. I'm sorry." He glanced at his watch. "It looks like I'm about two hours behind. I have two more people to meet with after Lawanna."

Because Gerrick's back was to Lawanna, she raised her eyebrows and made a happy face to Gina indicating that she was getting every minute of her time with him.

Gina swallowed a giggle. "That actually works for me because I could use another hour or so to go over my files."

"You want to meet at six then?"

"You don't mind working late?"

Gerrick laughed. "Honey, CEOs don't keep regular hours."

Though the way he called her "Honey" sent a ripple of excitement through her, Gina only smiled, nodded, and said, "I'll be back at six."

"Hey, Gina…" Gerrick called after her and Gina turned around.

"Rather than work in my office, why don't we go out to dinner?"

For a second, Gina stood frozen. Either her Gerrick really was back or the mean Gerrick had made two gigantic slips. First he called her "honey." Now he wanted to go out of the office to have their meeting in a more personal venue. He might not ravage her after dessert, but he was taking her somewhere they would be able to talk.

Suddenly things didn't seem as hopeless as they had only ten minutes before. Suddenly she felt that if she played her cards right she could actually get what she had been angling for in the first place. Just a chance for them to get to know each other.

She smiled. "Yeah, that sounds great."

"Good," he said and went back to work.

*  *  *

But while making the transition from Lawanna who seemed to want to stay and chat indefinitely, to Josh Anderson, Gerrick started to have second thoughts about dinner.

"Are you okay?" Josh asked about ten minutes into their discussion of the more intricate responsibilities of Josh's new position. "You seem distracted. If you would rather do this tomorrow, we can."

Gerrick shook his head. As Hilton had predicted, once he explained Gerrick's move and endorsed Gerrick's return, Josh, Ethan and most of the other employees had no problem with Gerrick coming on board as CEO. Everyone supported him. Josh and Ethan treated him as the friend he had been before his departure.

"No, I'm fine."

"Gerrick, it's after five. Go home. Rest. Your first full day is always the hardest. Don't overdo."

"It's too late for me not to overdo. I have two more meetings scheduled for this evening."

"At least tell me you plan to order out for supper."

"No… Well, I'm not ordering out. I asked Gina if we could hold our meeting at a restaurant."

Josh smiled. "Oh. Good idea."

*No, it wasn't,* Gerrick thought. It was a terrible idea. And it was a terrible idea for the very reason Josh was smiling. Eating dinner at a restaurant sent all the wrong messages…especially since they would be alone. If he wasn't careful the evening would feel more like a date than a business meeting.

"If you order out, who do you order from?"

Josh sighed. "Gerrick, don't change your plans. Get out of the office."

"I think the work will get done more quickly if we stay in. Then I can go to my hotel and get some rest. I know I shouldn't have jet lag, but I'm having some kind of trouble getting into the swing of things here. I'm tired. I would just love to get back to my room and go to bed."

Josh looked as if it pained him to answer Gerrick's question, but at the same time it would have pained him not to. "When I stay late, Olivia picks up something for me."

"Don't worry about it then. I'll find a place that delivers."

"No, don't," Josh said. "Olivia loves to do these things. Since we set back our wedding to make up for the time she lost staying with Gina while Hilton was in the hospital, she's now ahead of schedule, and looking for things to do."

Gerrick laughed at the exasperated tone of Josh's voice and then agreed to let him call Olivia and have her order something. The rest of their meeting went smoothly, as did the meeting they held with Nadine Bolivar, the person chosen to replace Josh in Public Relations and Advertising. It was clear Josh went out of his way to keep the discussions moving so that Gerrick could have a few minutes alone before his dinner meeting with Gina.

Gerrick relished the downtime. For a fleeting second he considered unrolling his shirtsleeves and slipping his jacket on again to make sure his meeting with Gina had the proper tone, but he changed his mind. He was tired. If anything, rather than put on his jacket, he thought he should take off his shoes and socks and put his tired feet up on the coffee table in front of the aging floral sofa.

He was chuckling at the thought when Gina entered his office wearing the peach-colored jacket of her suit and carrying her purse and his laughter died. Not because he forgot to tell her of their change of plans, but because she was so damned beautiful. Even dressed for work, she was incredibly sexy to him. He recognized that knowing what was under that suit had something to do with the way his heart always seemed to skip a beat when she entered a room and he acknowledged that he should stop thinking about it. But every time he saw her, the images came flooding back and he remembered everything about her...everything about making love to her. Unfortunately, he also knew that if he didn't stop thinking about that trip to Vegas, their kisses and their wedding night, she would drive him crazy.

"Oh, I'm sorry," he said, trying to sound calm and professional and not like a man still passionately in love with her. "I forgot to call you. Josh told me Olivia could order us dinner and deliver it. This way we could work in the office," he said, not really lying, but stretching the truth to construct an explanation that made the most sense. "So, if you want to take your purse and jacket back to your office, you've got a few minutes before Olivia gets here."

Gina's happy expression disintegrated. But she said, "Okay," and walked away.

When she was gone, Gerrick let out the deep breath he had been holding, and ran his hands down his face, knowing he had to stop having these flashbacks of making love to her and also knowing he had been right. She had completely misinterpreted going to a restaurant. He felt like a heel, but her reaction proved he had been correct. He couldn't take her out.

"Hey, Gerrick!" Olivia walked into his office and set a bag of sandwiches and two plastic containers of salad on the coffee table by the sofa. "Josh said you and Gina were working late."

"Yeah, thanks."

"Don't worry. This isn't a big deal. When I worked for Josh I got a lot of dinners for him because the cafeteria caterer leaves at two-thirty. I know how to get reimbursed from petty cash. And, really, it's not out of my way or anything."

"Thanks," Gerrick said, smiling his approval. Olivia returned his smile, but didn't make a move to leave.

"Something else?"

She shook her head. "No."

"Okay then…" Gerrick began as Gina entered the room.

Olivia stood grinning at her.

"Hi, Olivia."

"Hey, Gina. I brought dinner."

"Because we're *working* late," Gerrick said, deliberately accenting the word working. "And we appreciate it, but the longer you stay, the later we have to work tonight."

Olivia gasped. "Oh, gosh, I'm sorry!" she said and scrambled to the door. "Josh is waiting for me anyway."

"Good. Good night."

"Good night."

Gerrick waited thirty seconds after she was gone before he turned to Gina. "Sorry about that."

"About what?"

"About you missing a decent meal, about Olivia,

about you having to work late. I guess you could take your pick.''

"Like you said, CEOs don't have set hours.'' She took a seat on the sofa and opened the brown bag to get a sandwich. "I'm used to this.''

Relieved that she had adjusted and was okay with not going to a restaurant, he relaxed and sat beside her. For the first time since his return from Maine, he had a feeling that things could go back to normal if only because she was so comfortable. "I bet you are.''

She handed him the first sandwich she took out of the bag. "Because my dad could meet with me at home I was always the last person on his schedule. Lots of times we held our discussions in the car driving home.''

He laughed, then peered under the foil wrapping. "Oh, tuna.''

"I thought you liked tuna.''

"I love tuna. I had it for lunch.''

"Oh, that would be why I knew you liked it.'' She gave her sandwich to him. "This one's roast beef.''

"You're sure?''

She smiled. "Yeah. I'm sure. I like tuna, too.''

Their fingers brushed in the exchange and Gerrick clamped his mouth shut to keep from sucking in his breath. He had adjusted to being in the same room and even sitting on the same sofa, but he hadn't expected to touch her. He busied himself with his foil wrapper and the moment passed, but because of her reaction to not going out, he couldn't miss this chance to strengthen his position about their marriage. "I guess that proves we really don't know a lot about each other.''

"I disagree.''

She said it so confidently that he gaped at her. "How can you of all people say that?''

"Because I thought this whole relationship through twice. Once when I woke up that morning in Vegas and realized we were married and again yesterday. And both times I came to the same conclusion. By working together, having lunch every once in a while and talking after meetings we found out a lot about one another, even though we didn't date and we really didn't set out to get to know each other."

Gerrick almost grimaced. He had set out to get to know her. Specifically he had set out to integrate himself into her life. The result was he had fallen in love with her, while she didn't even realize they were getting acquainted until months later.

"Yeah, well, I give you that," he mumbled, then let the conversation fade away, because he was starting to feel things again. He supposed it was proximity, but every inch of his body seemed to be on red alert and he needed all of his concentration to keep himself from drifting closer on the sofa.

After a few minutes of silence and a few bites of sandwich, Gina said, "When I went back to my office because you were still with Lawanna, I wrote a report on most of my findings. If we're not going to talk, you could read that while we eat."

Gerrick felt a tad guilty about the fact that he couldn't even talk to her because he was so busy fighting off his attraction. But he nonetheless welcomed the report. If he read it now, they would get done quickly and he could get away from her.

Gina opened a folder and pulled out four or five computer-generated pages. She handed them to him with a smile, but rather than go back to eating, she found the remote control for the small TV on a bookshelf and turned on the evening news. She set the volume low enough that Gerrick could read while she watched.

Touched by her consideration, and feeling like a heel because he couldn't treat her normally, he lightly tugged a strand of her hair to get her attention. "You really are used to this, aren't you?"

She smiled. "Yes."

Her smile was so pretty and she was so comfortable that Gerrick realized how easily she fit into his world. But he reminded himself that it had been his goal to have her fit into his world. That was what he had been working toward for the six months before they got married. He knew he shouldn't make too much out of this ease between them because it was nothing but his plans coming to fruition. Except it was too late. He couldn't have her in his world.

Tired, confused, he read her report. Five minutes later, he whistled softly. "You're brilliant."

"Not really. I just know our people. It's my job."

"You're very good at it. And because of that, I think our meeting is over."

Puzzled, she turned to face him. "Really?"

"Yeah. Your report basically answers all my questions about the people I'm considering shifting around." Bracing his elbow on the back of the sofa and his head on his fist, he added, "Now I'll write a report giving you instructions and then you can act on them."

"Okay," she said, obviously pleased that her work had been accurate and efficient. She also leaned her elbow against the back of the sofa and her head on her closed fist, putting them face-to-face.

Gerrick's smile faded. He didn't know anyone who had the color of eyes Gina had. Violet. He didn't know anybody who had her smile, her unusual sense of humor, her gift of understanding people. He didn't know anybody he would rather be married to.

Hell, no woman ever even made him think about marriage until he met her.

As if guided by an unseen force, they began to drift together and Gerrick knew he was going to kiss her. He wanted to kiss her. Darn it! He wanted to do more than kiss her. He wanted to make love to her. And, technically, he was allowed.

Their faces drifted closer and closer. Gerrick could feel his heart beat. He could see her eyes cloud with desire as the space disappeared between them. This was what he wanted. It was what she wanted.

In the last second, Gerrick bounced off the sofa. "This isn't right."

Calm, casual, Gina leaned back. "Why not?"

"Because we've already decided we wanted to get a divorce."

"*You* decided we should get a divorce."

Gerrick spun to face her. "*You* told me to leave town a week after we were married! *You* told me you didn't remember the wedding. *You* told me the marriage was a mistake."

"I know. I was wrong."

He gaped at her. "You were wrong?"

She shrugged. "I was wrong."

He felt as if all the air had frozen in his lungs. Just like in Vegas when she proposed, everything he wanted seemed to be at his fingertips. But it had been a mirage then and could very well be a mirage now. "Don't do this."

"What? Don't admit that I like you?"

He squeezed his eyes shut. "Don't tempt me with something that I can't have."

"But, you see, Gerrick, that's where we disagree. I think if we took our time and did this right, we could have it."

Gerrick felt himself weakening. Really, really weakening. He saw the big house with the fence and the kids and the dog and like always he saw himself fitting into the picture. But he wanted it so much he knew better than to hang his hopes on somebody he couldn't trust.

And that was the real obstacle. He did not trust Gina. She didn't remember their marriage, regretted it in the morning, talked herself into it on the flight home, and talked herself out of it the week they were apart. Then she never contacted him the entire time he was in Maine, but once he was home she seemed to have changed her mind.

How could he trust her?

He blew his breath out on a long sigh and walked to his desk.

"Gina, the decision about the marriage is made." He caught her gaze not just to be sure that she heard and understood him, but also to prove to himself he could do this. He *had to* do this. "I can't go back. I'm sorry."

# Chapter Five

Gina arrived home and discovered her father was waiting for her. "Hey, Dad."

"Hey, Gina. Why so late?"

She tossed her purse to the foyer table beneath the mirror and dropped her briefcase by the spiral staircase so she wouldn't forget it when she went upstairs. "Gerrick is planning some employee restructuring. Actually, I think he's going to realign entire departments. I wrote a report."

"And it took you until now?" her father asked, leading her into their all-white living room, an indication that he wanted to talk.

Exhausted from a long day and frustrated with Gerrick, Gina didn't feel like socializing. But she had also nearly lost her dad when he had his heart attack, and he wasn't out of the woods yet. Time with him seemed more precious. More important. She would never be too busy or tired to talk to him again.

"No. I wrote the report, he read it while we ate in his office, and he told me I was brilliant."

Gina took a seat on the sofa and her father headed for the wet bar. "You are brilliant."

"Yeah, right, *Dad*. You're my father. You're supposed to think that."

"I'm not the slightest prejudiced. I've seen your work. You're a genius with people." He picked up a wineglass and waved it. "Want a drink?"

Because Gina hadn't yet straightened out the mess that resulted from her last bout with alcohol, just hearing the word wine made her stomach flip-flop. She quickly shook her head. "No thanks."

Her father took his time returning the glass to the rack, and Gina realized she had made a major mistake. He was too smart of a person not to recognize from her tone and her rapid reply that something was up. Gina knew it for sure when he asked, "Is there anything you want to talk to me about?"

She didn't want to insult him by not confiding. She also had a new appreciation for him since his heart attack, but there were some things wise daughters did not discuss with their fathers.

"No. There's nothing I need to talk about."

"You're sure?"

"Yes... No. I'm not sure," she said, suddenly realizing something so obvious she should have seen it before. Nobody knew Gerrick like her father did, and anybody who needed advice about dealing with him would go to Hilton Martin to get it. Of course, if that person had married Gerrick then dumped him, she doubted they would spill the whole story. Because Gerrick was one of Hilton's closest friends, they wouldn't really want to admit certain unpleasant details. Or maybe they wouldn't tell the real story at all, but make up something similar. A decoy. A story or scenario that would get the answer they needed without making themselves look like an idiot.

"Actually, Dad," she said, deciding she wanted her father's take on this and the best course of action to get it would be to steer clear of the truth and go directly for the decoy. "There are a few things I would like to discuss."

"I'm all ears," he said, leaning against the bar to give her his complete attention.

"I'm having a little problem with Gerrick," she said, careful to make herself sound professional and prudent, not like the employer's daughter squealing on her supervisor. "You won't think he's a bad CEO if I disagree with something he's doing?"

"No matter what you say I will always consider him a fabulous CEO. I worked with him for twelve years, remember? I know what he can do. I think it's possible the two of you could experience problems working together, but he's right where he should be. I won't think any less of either of you if you tell me there's a communications snafu. Now shoot."

"Okay," Gina said, appreciating his term "communications snafu" because that was exactly what they had. A communications snafu sounded fixable, workable, innocent. "The thing that has me the most confused is that he can be so sure about something one minute, then change his mind the next."

Unimpressed, Hilton stooped down to rummage

through the refrigerator beneath the bar. "That doesn't sound like Gerrick."

"I didn't think that was normal for him, either. But the thing we disagree on isn't a big thing. It's a little thing," Gina said, almost wincing at her lie because as far as she was concerned their marriage was the biggest thing that had ever happened to her. Lord knew it was the most confusing. But there was no reason for her father to know the size of this problem. It would only make him more curious, and more determined to ferret out details. "It was just something small that he changed his mind on, but in what seemed like a matter of seconds he went from being red-hot to being ice-cold."

Her father peeked up from behind the bar and frowned. "Red-hot to being ice-cold?"

"Let me put it another way," Gina said, not liking that analogy much herself because it brought all the wrong mental pictures to mind. Not the "ice-cold" part. Those pictures she could deal with. The "red-hot" part, unfortunately, conjured up the morning after her wedding, the red bra, the hanging panties. It propelled her mind in all kinds of inappropriate directions. And she was not pleased with her subconscious for slipping that in.

"Gerrick *thinks* he's changed his mind about this thing, but I don't think he has. I think he still wants to pursue the original course of action, but he won't."

"Then there's a good reason," Hilton said, leaving the bar and relaxing beside her on the sofa with a bottle of mineral water. "Gerrick never does anything without a reason. And once he hooks into a plan of action it's not easy to change his mind. He's got the discipline of a Himalayan monk.''

Gina frowned. Just like her hot-and-cold analogy hadn't pleased her father, hearing Gerrick had the discipline of a monk was not music to Gina's ears.

"For instance," Hilton continued, "if he wanted to lose weight, even if you pushed his favorite dessert under his nose, he would resist it." He took a sip of water. "Now, notice I said *would* resist it. Not could resist it. Could implies there was a choice. When Gerrick makes up his mind there is no more choice."

"Great!" Gina huffed, falling back against the sofa cushion because if her father was correct, there was no hope.

Her father peered at her. "I thought you said this was a little thing?"

"It is," Gina hastily assured him. "It's just something small. A difference of opinion."

"But it's an important difference of opinion."

"To me it is," Gina agreed. "Let's just say it's something I would like to implement."

"Oh," Hilton said, sounding like he had just now caught on. "And you want to know how to get your own way with him?"

Gina winced. "Don't make me sound like a spoiled brat."

"You're not a spoiled brat. You might have been spoiled as a child, but as an adult you work within the confines of adult rules. You're a grown-up now, Gina. And I respect you. I know that if you want to change Gerrick's mind about something there's a good reason."

"Thank you."

"You're welcome."

He shifted on the seat, took a sip of water and peered at her expectantly, but Gina didn't say a word. Finally he sighed and said, "So what do you want to change his mind about?"

"Nothing," Gina said, shaking her head because she couldn't give him details. Besides, he was supposed to be telling her how to deal with Gerrick, not getting involved with work, which was what he thought they were talking about. "The company isn't your concern anymore. I feel guilty for having dragged you in this far. Just give me a generic answer for ways to change Gerrick's mind once he digs in his heels, because I'm not going to give you an itemized account that makes you think about things you're not supposed to think about."

"All right. All right. *Dr. Brown*," Hilton said sarcastically. "The trick to getting your way with Gerrick is to make him think the decision is his. Which means you've got to bombard him with information so he sees your answer is right even before you actually present it."

Though most of that suggestion flew over her head, one thing stood out as being ridiculous in her situation. "Bombard him with information?" Gina asked, confused by how she would do that. Gerrick knew her whole life. What more could she possibly tell him? What more could he need to know?

"Okay, how about this," her dad said. "Entice him."

For the first time since they started this conversation, Gina remembered that she had always suspected her father knew about her impromptu wedding. If he did, that word choice could mean he was giving her real advice.

Afraid of how he might answer, Gina peeked at her father. "Entice him?"

"Entice him. Rather than overwhelm him with facts, give him a hint here and a hint there that your idea might be the better one. Lead him to your side like a sweet-smelling woman leads a man into the moonlight."

Gina stared at her father. Interpreted one way, that line was nothing but a business metaphor. Interpreted another, it was a clear, almost direct order to seduce his favorite employee…who just happened to be her husband.

She said only, "Hmmm."

"He is, after all a man. And you've gotta know three things about men if you're going to work with us. First, we like to be right. Second, we don't like to be told what to do. Third, we don't like weaklings."

"What do weaklings have to do with anything?"

"Negotiate from a position of strength," Hilton said, then he rose. "Don't go to Gerrick with an idea you want implemented acting like a timid little mouse. Make suggestions. Point out reasons your way works. Entice him. But do it like a champ. Remember *strategists* advise leaders." He kissed her forehead. "And strategists are bold. Daring. If you plan to stay on Gerrick's team, you're going to have to be daring."

Gina sneaked into her office before seven the next morning. After spending the night contemplating her father's instructions, she finally concluded he hadn't been telling her to seduce Gerrick, but she also knew he was correct to tell her to be bold and daring.

In the twelve years she had known Gerrick she had never been daring…yet she must have been daring in Vegas. And bold. And enticing.

And let's not forget passionate.

If the location of her undergarments the morning after their wedding was any indication, she had been passionate. *They* had been passionate. In fact, were she to guess, Gina would say they were *incredibly* passionate, which was probably why Gerrick now behaved so coolly around her. Passion gave life and vitality to a relationship, and in their case might have made it irresistible. To snuff out temptation, he had to ignore their passion.

That was why she had chosen to wear a red dress that fit as if it were made to flatter her figure and cologne specifically created to bring a man to his knees. It was time for a full-scale implementation of Operation Jackpot.

She walked to her desk, dialed Gerrick's extension and got his voice mail.

"Gerrick, this is Gina. If it's possible, I'd like to meet with you this morning." She paused. Pointedly. "But, you know what? If you're busy don't worry about me. I can be your last appointment of the day again."

She hung up the phone with a satisfied smile. She would bet her bottom dollar she would be in his office before ten, if only because memories of their last late-night meeting would have him doing everything within his power to assure they weren't alone again.

Which was exactly what she wanted. She wanted him

to see this dress early and remember it all day, but she couldn't be obvious about it. She had to make it look like she didn't care if she saw him now or later, so he wouldn't guess she had worn the dress for him. Her father might think she didn't understand strategies and subterfuge, but Gina was beginning to think she was pretty darned good at it.

As expected, her phone rang at exactly eight o'clock. Joanna's arrival time.

"Hi, Joanna."

"How'd you know it was me?"

"Wild guess," Gina said. "And also I left a message on Gerrick's voice mail that I needed to see him. I figured you would be calling to set an appointment."

"He can see you at ten."

"Ten it is," Gina said. She hung up the phone grinning and swiveled her chair in three complete circles. Clearly, this man was no match for her in a battle of wits.

She spent the morning pulling files from her cabinet and before she left for their meeting, she freshened both her lipstick and her cologne. She also gathered a huge armload of the folders she had assembled.

"Hi," she said, sounding harried as she walked into Gerrick's office. "I thought of some other things about your employee reorganization last night, pulled some files," she said, dumping them on his desk, "and realized we might be making a few bad moves with your choices."

Gerrick simply stared at her. She didn't know if it was the cologne, the dress or the seventy-plus files she had strewn on his desk, but something caught his attention because he couldn't stop staring. His eyes had widened as if he were in complete shock. His lips were parted and his jaw sort of hung.

She was putting her money on the dress.

"What?" she said, feigning ignorance of why he was dumbfounded. "Oh, I know. You like the people we talked about yesterday and you don't want to hear my suggestions."

"No," Gerrick said, then cleared his throat. "I'm all for suggestions. You know I'm not the kind of person who has to have his own way all the time."

She smiled. Sweetly. Prettily. She wasn't exactly going in for the kill, but it never hurt to remind him she was sweet and pretty. "Great. These are the people I'm suggesting you consider," she said, waving her hand in the direction of her spilled files.

He looked up at her. "You didn't write a report?"

"I thought we would talk about them first."

"But the report worked so well last night."

She frowned. He was right. That report had worked well the night before. It worked so well he didn't have to talk to her, and didn't have to stay with her very long.

He wasn't getting another report.

"Before I summarize seventy-five files—"

*"You want me to consider shifting seventy-five people?"*

"That's a rough estimate."

"That's too many people. Pick twenty," he said, sounding sure and secure and not at all dazzled by her beauty and charm anymore. "Summarize them and come see me tomorrow at…'' He looked at his calendar. ''Two in the afternoon.''

''But I really think we should look these over this morning.''

''I can't,'' Gerrick said simply. ''I have another meeting in ten minutes.'' He rose. ''I'll see you tomorrow.''

Drat!

Her father wasn't waiting at the door when she came home, and Gina raced up to her room so he wouldn't see her dress. She yanked the tight red thing off her body, ran into her bathroom to remove about one-third of her makeup and all of her cologne and jumped into a simple pink sheath. Then she hustled downstairs, grabbed her briefcase from the foyer and walked back the corridor to her father's den where she found him reading a book on perennials.

''Hey, Dad.''

''Hi, honey!'' He leaned back in his chair. ''How did it go?''

''How did what go?'' she asked innocently.

''The thing you were trying to change Gerrick's mind about?''

''Oh, that.'' She tossed her briefcase to the sofa on her way to the chair in front of her father's desk. ''We didn't really get into it. He wants another report.''

''Hmmm,'' he said, closing his eyes as he obviously thought this through. ''Hard to make him think it's his idea when you're writing a report, not talking.''

''I know.''

''So what are you going to do?''

"I'm not sure, this whole strategist thing is new to me."

"I know," her dad said. He closed his gardening book. "And that's my fault. I just let you run your department how you saw fit. Made do with the employees you found for me, took your recommendations on promotions and raises."

Gina stared at her dad. "Are you saying I did a terrible job and you let me?"

"I'm saying I never taught you to fight for what you wanted. I always gave you what you wanted because your assessments were always right on the money. So now when you're trying to make a point you're too subtle. You don't know how to fight for what you want."

Stifling a grimace thinking about her red dress, Gina said, "I thought the whole point of this exercise was to be subtle."

"No, the point is to try to make Gerrick think whatever you want is his idea. Then he won't see himself as *changing his mind*. He'll think he's *speaking his mind*."

"And how does that fit in with fighting?"

He sighed. "Gina, fighting is staying in the game. You have to forget you heard the word *no* if or when you hear it. You have to get your arguments in the first chance you get and then repeat them every opportunity after that."

"And you don't think I did that today?"

"I think you would be smiling right now if you had."

Gina couldn't argue that, so she didn't.

"Okay, I'm going to tell you one of my negotiating tricks, but I want you to swear you'll never share it."

"Scout's honor."

"I mean it, Gina. This is a biggie. You can't share it."

"All right, I won't," Gina assured him, eager to hear this because she knew it had to be good. With her father as successful as he was, a "Hilton Martin business tip" should have Gerrick eating out of the palm of her hand before close of business tomorrow.

"Okay. One of the things you can do to get an opponent to change his mind is to list your points as negatives but in such a way that he starts to see them as positives."

She stared at him. "That's it?"

"Yeah, that's it."

"I'm not even sure I understand it, let alone that it will work."

"Oh, it'll work," Hilton said, then steepled his fingers under his chin. "How do I explain this?" he murmured, as he pondered his next words. "Say you wanted Gerrick to…be your date for Josh and Olivia's wedding."

Gina gaped at her dad. "What?"

"I know that's more personal than business, but trust me. It's the same principle." He tapped his fingers against his chin again. "We'll say you already asked him, but he said no. So the next day, you say, 'You know what, Gerrick, you were right. It would have been wrong for us to go to the wedding together. First off, people would think we were dating. And wouldn't that be awful. I mean, really, would you want to be dating me...."'"

Gina frowned. Her father's choice of example was bad enough, but now he was treading on sensitive territory. Did her father really think that dating her would be awful?

"He would have to be incredibly rude to agree with you," her father continued, obviously not seeing her frown. "So, he says something like 'That wouldn't be so bad.' And you say, 'Don't be silly. Our dating would just cause too many problems. It wouldn't be worth having to deal with all the people asking questions about what it was like to date me.'"

Gina said, "Hmmm."

"Are you getting the picture?"

"Sort of," Gina said, totally confused now because once again she couldn't tell if he was giving her real advice or making up a contrived example. Particularly since she could see what he was saying. It made sense for her to do exactly as he was telling her to do. She wouldn't even have to ask Gerrick to go to Olivia and Josh's wedding. There were hundreds of ways she could put this strategy into a conversation.

Whether he'd planned it or not, her genius dad had just given her the perfect suggestion.

He rose from his desk. "You mull that over while we go out to dinner."

"Is the cook off?"

"I gave her the night off. She's been doing double duty learning how to prepare fat-free meals, shopping like a fanatic and throwing away cookies and chocolate. I thought she deserved it."

Gina laughed. "Maybe if the cook would stop throwing away the chocolate, I wouldn't be so stressed."

Hilton put his arm around his daughter's shoulders. "Maybe if you would figure out how to deal with Gerrick you wouldn't need chocolate."

Realizing it was the red dress that probably got her evicted from Gerrick's office the day before, Gina decided against an overtly sexy and alluring outfit, and wore an understated, but attractive pale-purple suit that brought out the color of her violet eyes. She kept herself scarce all morning, and at two o'clock in the afternoon walked into Gerrick's office like a normal Human Resources director for their scheduled appointment.

"I have your report." She smiled and handed it across his desk.

He glanced up cautiously. After he checked out her outfit, which she knew was nice, but sane, he returned her smile. "Thanks."

"I still think we should talk about it."

"Okay, just have a seat while I read it."

*Bingo.* Just as she suspected. He couldn't handle their chemistry, or reminders of their passion. Which meant it must have been explosive, powerful and wonderful. And definitely worth fighting for.

"Okay," she agreed, and sat on the captain's chair across from his desk. "I see you aren't making much headway on redoing your office."

He looked up. "No, I'm not."

"I would be willing to help you…"

"That's quite all right," he said, returning his gaze to the report.

"It wouldn't be any bother."

"I'm fine for a few weeks."

"I'm sure you are but I just thought… Oh, I get it," Gina said, changing tactics by switching to her dad's advice because she suddenly realized it fit. "I'm sorry. I won't mention your office again. I should have caught on to this myself."

At that he frowned and peered up at her again. "Should have caught on to what?"

"Well, that you wouldn't want me…of all people…helping you redo your office. Think of the gossip that would start."

He returned his attention to her report. "I'm not worried about gossip."

"Really?" she asked, but didn't give him a chance to answer. "I would have never guessed that. In fact, I was assuming that being cautious—not really afraid but cautious—about appearances was part of why you didn't even want to try dating."

"That's not even close."

"Really? Because that was high on my agenda of reasons why we're not a good match. Of course, I have to worry that one of the people hearing the gossip is my father, so maybe it is a higher priority for me than for you."

"I'm sure that's it."

"Now that I think about it, I can see that you would have bigger concerns than gossip." He didn't say anything, so Gina plunged on. "I mean, really. Would you want to answer questions about how it felt to date the boss's daughter? I don't think so. That kind of embarrassment isn't balanced out by a few kisses." She

paused long enough for him to absorb that image, then
added, "It's probably not even worth passionate sex."

Gerrick seemed to freeze. This time when he looked
up at her he was frowning and might have even been
gritting his teeth.

"I'm sorry. You're trying to read and I'm just bab-
bling." She motioned with her hand for him to get back
to reading, but inside she was secretly pleased. He re-
acted every time she hit the right button. He couldn't—
absolutely couldn't—claim indifference. "You go
ahead. I'll be quiet."

"I have a better idea. Why don't you go back to your
office? I'll read this tonight and you can meet me tomorrow." He looked at his day planner. "At ten," he
added, then went back to work, plainly dismissing her.

Drat again!

For as much as it was really great to confirm their
passion, it was equally annoying to continue to prove
that every time she reminded him of said passion he
would kick her out. The purpose wasn't to get him to
remember he liked her. The purpose was to get him to
remember he liked her enough to forget all the reasons
he shouldn't, and do something about it!

Oh, well, at least she got to come back tomorrow.


"You shouldn't have talked while he was reading,"
her father said that night at dinner.

"You're the one who told me to talk."

"Yeah, but he doesn't like people who talk while
he's trying to read."

"Thanks."

"Gina, I'm not quite sure what you're doing wrong here. This was a simple straightforward mission."

Gina averted her eyes to her peas.

"And Gerrick's a man who listens to reason. What could you possibly be trying to get him to do that it's taking you three days to change his mind?"

"Just a couple of staff shifts," she said, then hid her grimace behind a forkful of potatoes.

"Well, stop being wishy-washy. Get out a sledge-hammer and pound your points home."

"Dad, are you going to remember this stuff when Gerrick gives me an unflattering performance appraisal?"

"I'm guessing that if you would get off your duff and make him listen to reason you wouldn't have to worry about your next performance appraisal."

Feeling as frustrated as her father, Gina realized it was time to bring out the big guns and she knew exactly what those big guns were. She wound her hair into the same kind of tight bun she had worn for gambling in Vegas, forgot all about the cologne her father suggested and used the shower gel she had purchased in the hotel store, then dug out the red sweater and taupe slacks she had found on the floor of Gerrick's hotel room. If something about this outfit pushed him over an edge, she had no qualms about wearing it.

"Good morning, Gerrick," she said, announcing herself at his office door two minutes after he arrived because she was tired of waiting.

"Good morning, Gina," Gerrick said cheerfully as

he turned from hanging his suit coat in his closet. But Gina watched his face freeze in place when he saw her.

She marched into the room and set another report on his desk. "You will love the findings in this."

He cleared his throat. "You know, I hadn't intended to be so quick about these changes. I'm thinking maybe…"

Bingo again. His way of dealing with her was to ignore her every time she reminded him that he liked her, or that he was attracted to her…or that they were married. He intended to kick her out again now, but this time Gina wasn't going to let him. "Nonsense. Just read what I wrote."

He drew a sharp breath, walked to his desk and grabbed the report as he sat. Gina paced the room, ostensibly to look bored while he read, but really to get herself positioned closer to him. She ambled from the front of his desk to the window behind the desk and then turned and said, "No questions?"

"I'm not quite done."

He didn't even look at her and Gina recognized he had totally shut her out, so she paced beside his chair, leaned in and pointed at an underlined paragraph.

"I thought this idea was particularly interesting."

Gerrick didn't say a word. She couldn't tell if he was ignoring her to continue reading, if the Vegas scent she had worn immobilized him or if her proximity was killing him. Whatever it was, she didn't budge. Didn't breathe. The next move had to be up to him.

Finally he said, "That is interesting."

He said it so slowly and cautiously that Gina glanced at him. Because she was bent at the waist and leaning over his desk, she looked directly in his eyes. She saw confirmation of the passion she knew must have led them to a wedding chapel in Vegas, but she saw that wasn't the only emotion in his beautiful green orbs. For the first time since their trip to Nevada, she saw something else. Something more subtle.

"I would have never thought to try Dolly and Deb in Quality Control," Gerrick continued, but his voice was a soft whisper.

"They're both detail people," Gina said, then licked her suddenly dry lips. For five quarters like some slot machines required, she would kiss him. In fact, she would bet that if she shifted closer right now, she wouldn't have to kiss him. He wouldn't be able to resist kissing her.

But she could still see that odd something in his eyes. Not exactly fear, definitely not cowardice, but more like caution…or pain. As if he knew what they could be getting into, but he also knew there were consequences. Unpleasant consequences.

She didn't know what put that caution there. But it made her angry to think that someone had hurt him. Actually, it made her furious. At that moment, she realized something with such startling clarity it almost took her breath.

She loved him.

It infuriated her that someone had hurt him. She wanted to comfort him. She wanted him to be happy. She wanted to make him happy. Not for any selfish reason. Not even for all the logical reasons she had thought of for them to remain married. Not even for the passion…which she still hadn't really experienced, and only got hints about from his reactions to her.

No. She wanted to make him happy because she loved him. And if he wasn't committed to loving her, as he was very clearly saying every time he rejected her, then she didn't want to get involved with him. Because he would hurt her.

She pulled away, walked around his desk, sat on one of the captain's chairs and took a long breath to refocus her thoughts. "I think you're also going to like my suggestions about Georgiann," she said, completely shattering the moment, changing the subject and stopping them both before they did something for which he wasn't ready.

The next move had to be his.

# Chapter Six

Monday morning, Gerrick awakened in a cold sweat. He bounced off the pillow, sitting straight up in his bed and stared blindly at the empty wall in front of him. He had just had a dream about his wife that would have killed a lesser man, but he knew why. He'd kept himself busy with work all weekend so he wouldn't have time to think about his personal life, but right before bed Sunday night he realized he would be seeing Gina again in a few hours. That set off a chain reaction of emotions that culminated in a dream so filled with longing his body still vibrated with need.

But the problem wasn't the dream itself. The dream was just a vehicle to show him that the real complication of this situation was that he did think of Gina as his wife. Every day she got bolder and more relaxed with him, more like the woman he had married in Vegas, the woman he knew she was when she left the office each afternoon. And every day he thought of her more and more as his wife and partner, and less and less as his co-worker and subordinate.

He combed his fingers through his hair. He was in deep trouble.

Unless she was right.

If there really was a chance that their getting married hadn't been a mistake, if she had only pushed him out of her life because of the shock of her father's heart attack, then he wasn't in trouble. He was exactly where he should be. Firmly in love with the woman he had married.

Unfortunately, no matter how relaxed and comfortable Gina was around him, or how interested and aggressive she had been of late, he knew she wasn't as sure about her feelings for him as he was about his feelings for her. When he returned from Maine she used words like "might" and "try" and "date" and to Gerrick those words didn't demonstrate much of a commitment. Yet, she had no fair way of proving a commitment unless they did try to have a relationship.

He cursed and jumped out of bed. Technically, they had already done that and it had failed. Though it was true she could have been panicked when they returned home and discovered her father was gravely ill, it was also true that at the first sign of trouble, Gina bailed out on their marriage. She didn't want his help or his support. She wanted him gone. And she had told him to leave.

He didn't feel that the odds of trying again were good.

But the odds of his keeping his sanity were even slimmer if he continued to pretend everything was fine. Because it wasn't fine. They were married. And he wanted to be married. Now she seemed to want to be married, too...or at least to date. Which should have been what they were doing at this point, anyway.

Except he had jumped the gun. *He* set them up to meet that Friday night. *He* took her to Vegas. *He* leaped on her marriage proposal knowing she hadn't had as much time as he had coming to terms with the fact that they were falling in love. *He* wouldn't let her tell him she was having second thoughts the morning after.

So now, in fairness, he couldn't sweep their marriage under the rug and pretend it hadn't happened. He had to deal with it. He either had to get tough, be strong and hurt himself and Gina by pulling away so soundly neither one of them would have another second thought, or he had to roll the dice one more time.

He paused before stepping into the shower. When he phrased it that way, it didn't sound so bad. It sounded no different than watching Gina push the buttons on the slot machine. Like a game. A gamble. And Gina was agreeable. She had come a millimeter away from kissing him Friday morning and probably would have kissed him if he had given her any kind of sign that he wanted her to. All he had to do was tell her he would meet her terms and the game could begin.

He walked into his office tingling with anticipation and not all of it was the expectation of good things. She had hurt him once. She could hurt him again. He was setting himself up for the wound of a lifetime if this didn't work out. But he also knew he had to try. Except, this time there would be no setup, no trickery, no manipulations. This time both of them would go into this knowing exactly what they were doing.

"Joanna!" he called, tossing his black leather briefcase to his desk. "Page Gina, tell her I want her in my office immediately."

"Will do, Boss," Joanna called back.

Without thought for the work that awaited him, Gerrick forced himself to take his seat rather than pace in front of the big window like he wanted to. This was either the smartest thing he had ever done or the stupidest. There was no in-between with this decision.

"What's up?" Gina asked, stepping into his office. He motioned for her to close the door.

She did, then sat on the chair in front of his desk.

"I thought about what's been happening between us personally, and I think I might have been wrong," he said, taking Gina so much by surprise, she could only stare at him. "I know I came across as rude and maybe even insulting, and I want to apologize."

Not quite sure what was going on and not about to embarrass herself by making an inappropriate assumption, Gina said, "That's okay, Gerrick. I understand…"

He held up a finger to stop her. "No. You might have understood what I felt on Friday, but I thought this through this weekend and I—"

The phone rang and Gerrick cursed. In her head Gina cursed right along with him. Half of her was ready to jump for joy. The other half wasn't that optimistic. She'd seen that odd look in his eyes on Friday morning. Gerrick was a cautious man, not about to get hurt again. She couldn't leap to a conclusion on what he was about to say or she would be the one who got hurt.

He punched the speaker button. "I'm sorry, Joanna, I forgot to ask you to hold my calls."

"Okay," Gerrick's secretary chirped. "But you might want to take this one. It's Hilton."

Gerrick cursed again, then jabbed the button to get the call on the speakerphone. "Good morning, Hilton. What's up?"

"Nothing. Just calling to see if you need me, if you have any problems, if there's anything you would like to talk about."

"No. Not yet anyway," Gerrick said with a laugh. "Right now, I'm still getting organized. In fact," he said, glancing up at Gina. "Someone's in my office right now."

"Oh, no. It's not Gina is it?"

Gina held her breath, realizing her father didn't know he was on speaker and probably thought she had come into Gerrick's office to implement one of his "mind-changing" tactics. If he said anything or tried to plead her case he would ruin everything.

Gerrick unsuspectingly said, "Yeah."

"Then I'll let you go," Hilton said quickly and Gina let out the breath she had been holding, hardly believing her dad would give up so easily and wondering if his acquiescence was a trick. After all, he couldn't admit he knew about her marriage, yet he got her to talk about her relationship with Gerrick every night by letting her speak generically instead of specifically. Begging off the conversation might be a way of coercing Gerrick into talking. Especially since the conversation was about her. She had never known her dad to miss an opportunity to talk about her or meddle in her life.

"That's okay. We're fine. I'm sure Gina doesn't mind waiting through our discussion."

"I'm also sure Gina doesn't mind waiting for me," her father replied. "But I promised myself I wouldn't be a snoopy old man. Hovering when I'm not needed. Trying to run things when I should just back off."

Again, completely innocent, Gerrick said, "You're not intruding. You're certainly not hovering. I appreciate your advice and input."

Hilton said, "Hmmm..."

"I mean it," Gerrick assured him. "A call every now and then isn't out of line."

"This morning it might have been," Hilton said and the tone of his voice almost caused Gina's mouth to fall open. He was actually going to hang up without meddling.

"I said I wouldn't interfere and I'm not going to. I'll talk to you later, Gerrick."

"Okay," Gerrick said, but by that time Hilton was already off the line.

"Strange conversation," he said to Gina who smiled, so shocked by her father's restraint she could only think of one reason for it.

"My dad has been very peculiar since his heart attack. Some days it's like he's a different man. I know he's bursting with curiosity about...a communications snafu I'm having with one of our employees," she said. She interjected "communications snafu" into the slot where "our marriage" should have been, because she didn't want Gerrick to know that she was talking to her dad about their relationship. Or, worse, that her dad either knew about their marriage or had some very strong suspicions. "But he waits until I bring it up, and then he only speaks in the most vague terms. He never looks at the newspaper. He has four thousand fliers for fishing boats and the other day I actually found a pamphlet from a dating service in his study."

Gerrick burst out laughing. "You're kidding!"

Gina shook her head. "Nope."

Gerrick's phone rang again and he gave it an evil look. Gina did the same because the casual, normal conversation they were having was exactly what they needed to ease them into a positive discussion of their personal life.

He took a long breath and hit the speaker button again. "Yes?" he said, sounding more polite and more professional than Gina would have been.

"The new contracts with two of the subsidiaries are here," Ethan said. "I'm having my assistant make copies and ship them to your office. Normally, I read them and give Hilton my recommendations, but I thought that since this is our first time through this particular process, you might want to read them for yourself."

"I do," Gerrick said. Gina could hear in his voice that he was excited at the prospect of his first big negotiation for the company, however he glanced up at her and said, "But I'm really busy right now. I expect to be tied up for at least an hour. Get copies to me. I'll call you once I've read them."

"Okay."

Gerrick hung up his phone. "Where were we?"

"Honestly," Gina said with a laugh. "I have no clue. I think we were talking about my dad."

"Which is not what I wanted to talk to you about."

"No?" Gina said, her heart pounding in anticipation.

"No." He drew a long breath. "Gina, I thought a lot over the weekend about…"

His phone rang. This time Gerrick cursed in two languages. Gina almost joined him.

"What!" he yelped into the phone, not bothering to hide his irritation.

"Overnight deposit figures are in, Gerrick," Josh said, then he laughed. "A bit of trouble this morning?"

"No." Gerrick's head fell between his shoulders in defeat. From what little Gina had been told about the inner workings of Hilton-Cooper-Martin Foods, she knew Gerrick had to talk to Josh.

"Can I call you right back?"

"Sure," Josh said and hung up his phone.

"This isn't going to work," Gina said before Gerrick got the chance.

Gerrick smiled at her. "No. It isn't. We need to have a long personal talk and we aren't going to be able to do it here."

"Maybe that's a good thing." she said and watched his expression change as if it was the first time he realized they were in a building full of people, most of whom needed his attention and that wasn't exactly conducive to a personal discussion.

"I'm just about certain it is a good thing," he agreed. "And, in fact, it might also be a good thing that we have to meet somewhere later for another reason. Once I say what I have to say you're probably going to want time to think about it."

Her heart pounded, but she wouldn't let herself get confident without good reason. This didn't mean their marriage was fixed. She remembered the "something" she had seen in his eyes on Friday. She knew an important issue held him back. She wouldn't be so foolish as to think a weekend of thought had changed that. Plus, their marriage, such as it was, wasn't a good one. The only truly positive, honest step he could be about to suggest would be that they date.

"Sounds serious," she said, then held her breath and crossed all her fingers and some of her toes.

"It is." He paused and caught her gaze. "You were right last Monday. I was wrong. We went about our relationship backward and now we need to start over and when I say start over, I mean go back to the beginning. I think we need to date.''

*Jackpot.*

Gina's eyes widened and she struggled to believe what she had heard. ''You want to date?''

''Yes.'' Once the word was out of his mouth, Gerrick seemed to be overwhelmed with relief. ''Yes!'' he said and began to laugh. ''But we need to be very clear about what this means. We'll probably even want to set ground rules. That is if we both still want to date after we've hashed out this whole thing together.''

She gaped at him. ''And you thought we could do that in the office?''

He peered at her across his desk. Both of his eyebrows were raised in censure. ''At least I didn't wear a tight red dress and killer cologne.''

Gina winced. ''Touché.''

''So…'' Nervous, he tapped his pencil on his desk. ''Do you want to have dinner tonight?''

''And discuss dating ground rules in a restaurant? In front of God knows who? Gerrick, you know my father has friends everywhere. There's no telling who would overhear.'' She shook her head. ''I think we should meet somewhere a little more private.''

''What about my hotel room?''

''I don't think so.'' From what she had pieced together it was a hotel that had gotten them into trouble in the first place.

''I'll tell you what. I'll call the hotel today and get my room switched to a suite. That way we'll have a sitting room.''

''I don't know…''

''We can't go to your house because your dad *lives* there. We can't talk in public. We are running out of options. Unless you would like to call your dad and get one of his pamphlets for a boat?''

That made her laugh, and also reminded her that she liked this guy and trusted him. Compromising on this was a perfect way to prove that.

''No. That's okay. You're right. Besides, I'm sure I'll be spending more than my fair share of time on a boat soon enough.''

''Okay, then. I'll see you tonight at my hotel.''

''Okay,'' Gina said, rising cautiously. Not because she was still uncomfortable with talking in his hotel room, but because she didn't want him to realize how excited she was. She waited until she was out of his office, past his secretary's workstation, down the hall, behind the closed door of her own office and in her executive washroom before she yelped for joy.

She had done it! She had changed his mind! Well, not completely but at least he wasn't flat-out saying no anymore. They would talk and sort things out so there wouldn't be any more complications, mix-ups or misunderstandings.

She didn't think the idea of talking things out would thrill her, but it did. She felt all those strange feelings she had felt the morning her father announced Gerrick was returning. She wanted to fluff out her hair, spritz on perfume, be anywhere but in her office.

The more excited she got, the more wrong it felt to be sitting behind her desk reviewing worker's compensation statistics, so she took the afternoon off. She didn't know if going home early to get ready for the evening was a continuation of her father's suggestion that she ''make her points'' with Gerrick, or if she was simply too happy to think about something as mundane as insurance, but she didn't want to stay at work.

Stepping into the foyer of her father's huge home, she considered calling out to let him know she was there, but changed her mind. The whole day felt different, special and *private*. She wasn't yet ready to share it. Instead, she sneaked upstairs and filled her tub with bubbles. Happily nestled in the warm bath she dreamily began to recall every second in Gerrick's office that morning, grateful for the phone calls that caused him to realize they needed to meet away from Hilton-Cooper-Martin Foods. But instead of getting the warm fuzzy feeling she thought she would get when she remembered his capitulation, she finally realized the phone conversations were only part of the problem. Gerrick had been nervous. And not joyful. More like resigned. He wasn't tingling with anticipation over meeting her tonight. He was tense and filled with anxiety.

She sat up in the tub.

Maybe she didn't have as much to be happy about as she thought she did?

Sinking back under the water she tried to remember absolutely everything she could about their trip to Vegas, seeking a clue about why they never seemed to be on the same page emotionally. When he was ready, she was not. Now that she was agreeable, he was not. Of course, even as "agreeable" as she was now, she had some reservations. She didn't want to begin playing the role of Mrs. Gerrick Green tomorrow. She didn't want to move in with him. She wasn't exactly sure what she wanted, except that dating made the most sense.

On the other hand, Gerrick hadn't ever seemed to want to date. From what she could remember of their trip to Vegas, it was clear that he had set his sights on the whole enchilada. Thinking back to their plane ride home, she remembered the man was smitten. Ready to face her father—his boss—with the news that he'd eloped with his daughter. If this were a fairy tale she would say he had been ready to slay a dragon for her, because metaphorically he was risking his life for her—at the very least his career.

He'd liked her that much…

Wanted her that much…

And she really couldn't figure out why.

Of course, he remembered getting married, making love and whatever conversation they had afterward. She did not.

She lifted her foot from the tub and watched the bubbles slide to her heel, then drop into the water. She already knew she and Gerrick were a lethal kissing combination. Was it so much of a stretch to think that Gerrick skipped several normal relationship steps because making love had been…well, fabulous?

Just the thought made her shiver.

If that were true, her not remembering would be a slap to his male ego.

After all, he hadn't actually changed his mind about her until after she told him she didn't remember getting married or making love.

Hmmm…

In the end she decided that the reason they weren't on the same page emotionally was because he remembered making love and she didn't, but not because they were that good together and not because she had dented his ego, but because it changed something. Making love always did. So she had a choice, resign herself to the fact that they would be off balance until they made love again. Or force the issue.

Pondering that, she put on a pair of blue jeans and the pink top she had been wearing the day Gerrick returned because she liked the way she looked in them. She applied a little makeup, including a touch of blush, and fluffed her hair to her heart's delight. Enjoying herself. For once in her life not arguing with her feminine instincts.

Unfortunately, those same female instincts were telling her that forcing the issue was the right thing to do. If she could see how things had changed or what had changed when they made love, then they would be negotiating from the same level.

On the other hand, making love as a negotiating strategy didn't seem appropriate, either.

Of course, just their kisses were enough to put a sizzle in her blood. If he kissed her enough, or took them as much as one step beyond kissing, there might not be any decision to be made.

Lost in thought as she skipped down the stairs Gina didn't see her father waiting in the foyer until she was about three steps from the marble floor. Only then did she realize she never told him she had plans and wouldn't be eating dinner with him.

"Anything you want to talk about?" he asked without preamble as she slowed her steps on the spiral staircase and didn't take the last few stairs to the floor.

She shook her head. "No. Why?"

"Well, you came home early and spent the afternoon in your room. I'm not the kind of guy to be nosy, but Maria had her ear to the door and she said she thought you were crying."

Gina laughed. She should have known better than to think he would really butt out. He might have begged off the phone conversation that morning with Gerrick but it was probably because he didn't want Gerrick to see how much he interfered in his daughter's life. Undoubtedly, the conversation had only whet his appetite.

"You know, Dad, I'm the first to admit you've been really different since your heart attack. And nine chances out of ten, you're probably very bored. But the truth is, if Maria had her ear to my door it was because you asked her to. And she didn't hear me crying. She might have heard the water running into my bathtub. Which makes me wonder what I sound like when I cry. But I wasn't crying. I was pampering myself. Getting ready to go out tonight..."

Her father gasped. "You have a date?"

"No," Gina said automatically because she didn't have clearance from Gerrick to tell her father anything. But the lie immediately stuck in her throat. First because she had to start paving the way to tell her father about Gerrick. Even if this relationship/marriage didn't succeed, she was going to have to tell him something. If she had a few mysterious "dates" she could use them as a springboard to explain everything else.

And, second, she knew this constant denial wasn't right and might actually be part of the problem. She and Gerrick thought of each other as co-workers first and if they didn't start thinking of each other at least as friends, if not a couple, they would never straighten this out.

"Yes, I have a date," she said and felt as if a weight had been lifted off her chest until her dad asked, "With whom?"

Okay, now she had painted herself in a corner. But she didn't let that bother her. She didn't have to deceive her dad to keep her privacy. It wouldn't be the first time she told him to butt out. She smiled and sweetly said, "None of your business," before heading for the door.

"You be home at a decent hour!" Hilton said, watching her go.

For that she turned. "Dad, I'm twenty-eight," she said but she stopped when a wave of confusion rolled over her. She was twenty-eight and she had never given her father cause for worry. Though this was the wrong time to start since it would be foolhardy to scare a man who was recovering from a bad heart attack, she was an adult and crazy about the man to whom she was unexpectedly married. Yet aside from a couple of silly flirtations and vague conversations, she had never really done anything about it. She suddenly recognized that just like with seeing them as a couple, if she didn't soon take a real step to make some kind of concrete commitment, this relationship would never go anywhere.

That could also be why Gerrick remembering making love and her not remembering making love was such a big deal. Making love was the seal of the marriage. The commitment. *He* had made the commitment. *She* had not.

She retraced the few steps that separated her and her father, kissed his cheek, then patted the spot she kissed before saying, "Don't wait up."

With that she walked out into the beautiful Georgia evening. The April temperatures already bordered on sultry. The scent of blossoms filled the air. And she was on her way to meet Gerrick. She could have said it aloud. She wanted to shout it from a rooftop.

She *loved* him.

And she was happy, no, excited, because she was going to make that commitment.

Gerrick was equally excited, though he wished they had just decided to go to the movies. There was plenty of time to discuss their relationship and maybe set some ground rules, and by doing it tonight they had ruined their first real date.

Date.

He was married to this woman. He had been courting her for months. They had spent a weekend together. He had made love to her. They had kissed a hundred times while she gambled. It seemed odd to date.

Except when he reminded himself that she hadn't picked up on the fact that he had been flirting with her and getting to know her for months, and didn't remember the rest of it. For her this was all brand-new and that was the problem. Gerrick was light years into this relationship and Gina was only beginning.

Because he needed to move his belongings from his original room to the suite, Gerrick had also left the office early. He ordered a bottle of wine and had it sitting on the low table in front of the pale-print sofa. He had nerves in his stomach the likes of which he had never experienced before, and six times he had debated straightening his tie and putting on his jacket again. He had no idea if he should dress casually or formally, no idea what Gina would be wearing. He did take it as a good sign that she had left work before noon, then he worried that she had taken the afternoon off because she couldn't handle inadvertently bumping into him in the hall, knowing they would be seeing each other tonight.

By the time she knocked on his door, he was a nervous wreck. He took three long breaths, straightened his tie and opened his door to her, only to discover she wore jeans and a simple shirt. Her hair was loose and free. She looked refreshed, invigorated and energetic, as if she'd spent the afternoon relaxing in a spa.

"I should have changed."

She smiled at him. "No. You're fine. You might want to loosen your tie, though," she suggested then reached up to do it for him.

Shivers of awareness skittered through him at the brush of the tips of her fingers against his neck. He almost grabbed them and brought them to his lips, but remembered he was so far ahead of her in this relationship that she might never catch up, and he stopped himself.

"I got some wine and we can order room service," he said, stepping away from her. "Or, if you would like," he suggested uncertainly, "we could do something simple like go to a movie. You know. Relax. Get comfortable with each other before we have this big discussion."

She glanced around the front room of his suite as if taking inventory, then she turned and smiled. "No. This is fine."

Seeing her in his room, among his things, the way she had been that morning in Vegas caused excitement to knot in the pit of his stomach, but Gerrick ignored it. He knew he was dealing with months of pent-up frustration. He didn't think it strange to be having these thoughts and feelings now. But he did know he had to control them.

He poured a glass of wine for each of them, then directed her to sit on the sofa. She took the glass from his hand and asked, "So where do you want to start? Did you come up with any ground rules?"

"To tell you the truth I've been too distracted to think about ground rules."

"That's right," she said, then sipped her wine. "You're in a new job."

"The job has nothing to do with it," Gerrick said with a laugh. "I could do this job in my sleep."

She peeked at him over the rim of her glass. "What's distracting you, then?"

"You... Us," he admitted because he knew they had to start being completely honest or they wouldn't stand a snowball's chance in hell. "I want to jump ahead to tomorrow and have to keep reminding myself to slow down because we're not on the same page emotionally."

She set her wine on the table. "I know," she said then scooted closer on the couch and Gerrick's heart skipped a beat. "We are in two different places emotionally and I think I figured out why."

"You have?"

"Yes, but that's not important. Right now," she said, sliding a little nearer, "I think it's more important for me to tell you that I have *always* thought you were very cute."

He looked at her askance. "Cute?"

"I was sixteen when I met you."

He smiled at the memory. "Yes, you were."

"And you were cute."

"Thanks."

"Now, I think you're very handsome." She reached out and laid her palm on his cheek. "And what I would like to do more than anything else in the world is make love with you."

He caught her roving hand. "Don't. I don't think that's a very good idea."

"Actually, I think it's the best idea either one of us could have. I think it's why we're really on different pages. In fact, I think it might be the answer to our communications snafu.''

As she said the last, Gina eliminated the distance between them and kissed him.

# Chapter Seven

Gerrick cupped the back of Gina's neck and brought her closer as if he couldn't resist what she was offering. He plunged his tongue into her mouth and kissed her with a ferocity that spoke of pure male hunger. Pent-up desire. Long denied needs. Things he couldn't hold back anymore.

Though Gina collapsed against him, weak with the same physical longings, she managed to keep a slim hold on objectivity and began to understand what Gerrick felt. He hadn't rushed into their Vegas marriage because he logically recognized that they knew each other and would make a lovely couple, but because they were passionate about each other. And if she wanted him that was how she would reach him. With passion not logic.

She gave the slightest push on his chest, and Gerrick fell backward, taking her with him, kissing her the whole time. His tongue mated with hers. His lips nibbled and caressed hers. But most of all his mouth never left hers as if he couldn't get enough of her. He wanted her. He needed her and he couldn't hide it.

Gina reveled in it because this hunger was actually what she wanted, too. If he had kissed her like this while they were playing the slots she could completely understand why she hadn't wasted a second in marrying him. He was a good, decent man filled with passion…for her. Not her money. Not her position in the community. Not the things he could be, have or do because of being married to her, but because of *her*. A man couldn't fake passion like this.

Their positions shifted several times on the sofa, as their kisses grew hot and stormy. His hands raced and roamed along her arms and back and eventually skimmed her breasts. Both of them froze.

"This isn't going to work."

Gina knew Gerrick meant that kissing wouldn't lead them into the productive discussion they were supposed to be having, but she deliberately misinterpreted him and answered as if he were complaining about the cramped sofa. "Then we should probably move to the bed."

He looked at her, searching her eyes, his green orbs probing deeply. "Really?"

"Yes. Gerrick, I love you."

She surprised them both by saying it, but she wouldn't take the words back because she knew they were true, though she only now grasped how it had happened. For years she'd loved him as a friend. She had more than appreciated his support as a co-worker. She had relied on it. He was someone she knew she could count on, especially after Chad left her. In Vegas when they had discovered their chemistry, they had shifted from friends to lovers. All the good things they had shared culminated as love. For Gina it was that simple.

Gerrick rolled off the sofa and reached down to pick her up, carrying her to the next room and gently laying her on the center of the bed. He kicked off his shoes and sat on the edge to remove his socks and Gina pulled her shirt over her head. She toed off her loafers. She unsnapped her jeans. By the time he got rid of the layers of clothes he wore to be CEO of Hilton-Cooper-Martin Foods, Gina was naked, waiting for him.

"You are so beautiful," he whispered reverently, confirming all the conclusions Gina had been making as they kissed. He couldn't fake this. She had seen other men feign passion for her too many times not to be able to recognize the real thing when it came along.

She opened her arms.

He nearly fell into them, the fingers of one hand twining into her hair, while his other hand slid around her waist to pull her against him. He rolled once until they were side by side on the bed, then his lips roamed along her jaw, down her neck, across her collarbone and down her entire right side. If the caress hadn't been so erotic, she might have giggled at the tickling, but it was erotic. And sensual. The speed of it only added to the intensity, the frenzy, the need.

The lights of Atlanta danced behind the sheer white curtain covering the only window in the room. Their limbs made a rustling sound against the bedspread. But neither one of them stopped to notice. Gerrick was fire and speed, need and hunger and Gina wanted every second of it. She touched him and kissed him and opened for him.

But where she had thought this initial burst of passion would be quick and wild, probably as their wedding night had been, Gerrick unexpectedly slowed the pace, the rhythm. He kissed and caressed her, whispering words of love that mesmerized her. Until she realized that they were staring into each other's eyes, locked together as if by some invisible force. Everything inside her pulsed with need.

Then something seemed to click for him and he changed again. The tempo increased, the words of love ceased, but he held her gaze, waiting with her for the climax that hit them almost simultaneously. And she saw in his eyes confirmation of everything she wanted to believe.

This man loved her. Maybe even more than she loved him.

"I thought we were going to take it slow," Gerrick said, wrapping his arms around her and pulling her to nestle against him after he tossed the comforter from the bed and covered them with the sheet.

"We are."

"And this is your idea of slow?" he asked, indicating the twining of their naked limbs beneath the cool white sheet.

"Yes."

"Gina..." Gerrick said, his voice a low growl.

"All right. I confess. I sort of thought I—we—needed to get that out of the way."

"Get what out of the way?"

"Let's face it, Gerrick. You remembered making love and I didn't. As far as I was concerned your memories sat between us like a third person. I knew you knew something I didn't know. Something that made you feel more strongly, more sure than I felt. And I guessed it was something good." She reached up and smoothed her palm against his unshaven jaw. "I was right."

He laughed. "Oh, yeah? And what was this good thing that I knew but you didn't?"

"That we're incredibly passionate about each other." She stretched like a cat, fighting a purr, and snuggled against him. "I must have gone one step over the tipsy line in Vegas at about the same time that our chemistry started to click. So you remembered it. Wanted it. But I wasn't reacting like the woman you married."

He rubbed his hand down her arm. "I suppose that's one way to put it."

"But now I'm caught up and I see why you had all the feelings you had." She shrugged. To her this was a simple, easy equation with no conclusion to be drawn other than that they needed to be married. "We're passionate about each other."

"I would go to the ends of the earth for you." He pulled her away from him so she could see his eyes. "I would do anything you wanted. You will never have to doubt me."

If his fierce expression was anything to go by, Gina knew that was true. She smiled. "We're simple people, Gerrick. There are no dragons to be slain in our world. I don't even have a halfway decent enemy."

"No, but there is a little matter of telling people we're married."

"There is that," Gina said, then sighed. "So what do we do?"

Gerrick lay back on his pillow and stared at the ceiling. "The first thing we were going to do when we got back from Vegas was tell your dad." He glanced at her. "And at the time it made sense, but right now it doesn't."

"It doesn't?"

He shook his head.

"Why doesn't it?"

"Because as much as I think I love you, Gina, I have to agree with your assessment that we're passionate about each other."

"And this is bad because…"

"Because it clouds our judgment." He laughed lightly. "Talk about an understatement."

Gina thought about that for a second, and realized that he might be right. Proving their passion hadn't solved their problem, because Gerrick didn't seem to be caught up with her logic. While she was racing around the day after their wedding, thinking things through, trying to justify getting married and eventually even justifying staying married, Gerrick was rolling with the good times. So though she was currently caught up to his level of passion, he wasn't with her in the logic department.

Contrary to her original belief, they weren't dealing with a simple equation. They had a two-part problem. And they were only halfway through it.

"I see what you're saying."

"Do you?"

"Yeah, I do," she said, pushing herself up on her elbows so she could study his face. "I more or less thought this through twice and both times I came to the same conclusion. We're made for each other. But you haven't really thought it through." She grimaced. "Well, you thought you were thinking it through, but the first time you were justifying going to bed and the second you were trying to talk yourself out of it. But you couldn't." She smiled. "Because you like me."

"I more than like you. I love you completely and forever, but I have to wonder if we can live together."

Because that was the one thing Gina was sure they could do, she laughed.

"This won't be so funny when you realize I'm overprotective and demanding."

She stared at him. Good-natured Gerrick thought he was overprotective and demanding? "I find that hard to believe."

"My father left my mother and me when I was six. My mother later abandoned me with her childless sister," Gerrick said, again shifting so he could see her as he spoke. "In a way, I think it was as much of a gift for me to be raised by my aunt as it was a gift to my aunt to get to raise me. But my mother never told either of us what was happening. She dropped me off for the summer then never came back. My aunt and uncle took it in stride, got my birth certificate and enrolled me in school, but I went through a lot of confusion, four years of rebellion and four years of trying to make up for the rebellious years." He drew a long breath that he blew out on a sigh, as he lay on his pillow again. "I succeeded and they even got to see me graduate from college, but then they were killed."

"Right before you came to work for my father?" Gina asked with a gasp.

"Yes."

She rubbed her hand across the hair on his chest. "That's a hell of a life story."

"Yes, it is."

"And very different from mine."

"Exactly."

"And also why you think we're going to have trouble living together."

"Our pasts make us who we are and also determine how we react to things."

Trying to understand how he had formed that opinion, Gina's brow furrowed. "Are you saying my past dictated that I would reject you when I got home from Vegas and discovered my dad had a heart attack?"

"Yes. But that's a bad example. I think the real problem is me not you. Though your mother died, you've never doubted that she loved you. And any idiot can see that your father worships the ground you walk on. I don't want to say you never had troubles, but they weren't like mine."

"No, they weren't, but I had my problems," Gina said, surprised at how proud she sounded to have had trouble in her life. "I've had relationship problems that might not rival being abandoned by your parents, but have taught me I need to be careful with people. And I guess in my own way I could be overprotective and demanding, too."

"So, even though we come at it from two different approaches, for opposite reasons, you think we're both overly careful." Gerrick rubbed his hand down her arm.

"I wouldn't say that, but I would say that neither one of us would enter into this lightly."

There was a moment of silence before Gerrick said, "Aside from Chad, the ingenue-dating womanizer, what other relationship problems did you have?"

"The usual," Gina said with a shrug. "I mostly dated guys who wanted my money, or access to my dad's money. You would be surprised how many investment bankers get my number from a friend who thinks we would be perfect for each other."

Gerrick laughed.

"It's not funny."

"Of course it is, if only because we're so damned opposite. Your problem is that everybody wants you. I was deserted. Twice. People probably pay good money to get your phone number, seats beside you at the symphony or the table next to yours."

"And you think that's fun?"

"I'm sure it's not," Gerrick said, obviously trying to be serious, but he didn't make it because he laughed. "Still it does underscore that we're very different. And our experience of life can't be compared."

"Then let's not compare it. Why don't we live for today and tomorrow and just forget about the past."

"Because the past shapes us. There's bound to come a point or a problem that will cause one of us or both of us to react in a way the other one doesn't expect. Like when we returned from Vegas and discovered your father had a heart attack."

She almost argued that she refused his help that day because they hadn't told anyone they were married and she wasn't prepared to address it, but she knew that was only part of it. "I guess."

"So I'm suggesting that we need to take it slow."

"Well, you better not want to take it too slow because I'm just about certain my dad suspects."

"Your dad knows we're married?"

"I think he just suspects. Otherwise, I'm sure he would confront us," Gina said, remembering how her father couldn't seem to get off the phone quickly enough once he realized she was in the room with Gerrick. "The way I have this figured out, he must have realized there's a reason we haven't made the announcement, and he's afraid that if he interferes he might screw things up, so he's staying away."

Gerrick sighed his understanding. "Ah… That was what was odd about the conversation this morning."

Gina nodded. "Exactly. And if we tell him, there will be no reason for him to stay out of our business anymore and he might just make our lives miserable."

"Or force issues we don't want to be forced."

"So we can't tell him."

"Which means we can't tell *anybody*," Gerrick said unhappily.

Deciding they had had enough serious discussion for one night, Gina stretched against Gerrick. "I can make it worth your while to keep the secret for a bit." She pulled his face down for a long open-mouthed kiss.

"I'm listening," Gerrick whispered against her mouth.

Gina laughed. "I think keeping this a secret could be lots of fun."

"Like how?"

"We could find all kinds of silly excuses to leave work and come here."

"I love leaving work."

"Hey, you're not supposed to tell me that! I'm the person you're trying to earn money for."

"I don't care," Gerrick said, as he rolled her over and kissed her neck.

They made love again. This time a little slower and punctuated with more words of love than Gina had heard from one man in an entire relationship. For that reason alone, she didn't think this was going to end. There was no way on God's green earth people this passionate about each other could possibly have an unresolvable problem.

But she also understood Gerrick's caution. Being blinded by lust had kept him from seeing the logic. She was head and shoulders ahead of him in understanding why they were good for each other, and just as she had to catch up to him in the passion department, now he had to catch up in the logic department.

Though she hated leaving him to go home, she knew that Gerrick needed time to think all this through and it was better for her not to be there while he thought. He walked her to her car in the hotel parking lot. Amid a flurry of kisses and whispered wishes that she could stay, Gina left Gerrick and headed for her father's house.

She sneaked in the front door, only to discover her dad, the famous Hilton Martin, man who did his own commercials, had just retired from running an enormous conglomerate and was renowned for making grown men cry in negotiations, pacing like the father of a teenager.

"Where have you been?"

Gina only stared at him. "In the first place, it's only a little past midnight, not late enough for you to be panicked. In the second, I'm twenty-eight. If I would have chosen to stay out all night, that would have been my business. And in the third, I told you not to wait up."

He said, "Hmmm," as if he desperately wanted to comment on the subject and Gina decided to let him stew awhile. She didn't know how he had found out about her and Gerrick and really didn't know how much he knew. But she did see this was a better way to occupy his thoughts than the four thousand boat brochures, worries about his upcoming surgery or the dating service.

She kissed his cheek and bounded up to bed content. Not only was her love life keeping her father out of trouble, but she had a love life. A real love life. For the

first time ever, she was with a man who loved her for
her, not for her family name, her position or her money.
Gerrick loved her. Just the thought made her giddy.

The next morning Gina was standing in the reception
area of Hilton-Cooper-Martin Foods talking with one of
the union employees about benefits when Gerrick arrived at work. She glanced up and smiled, and Gerrick
returned her smile before greeting John Wilson.

Gina was glad he drew Wilson's attention away from
her because that smile alone made her catch her breath.
As Gerrick calmly walked away, she wondered how
long they could realistically keep their relationship a
secret. Especially since she was ready to swoon from a
facial expression. Yet watching him confidently stride
to his office she knew she would only have to worry
about herself. Gerrick seemed better able to handle this
than she was.

However, as Gerrick virtually flew past his secretary,
he barked, "Get Gina Martin into my office immediately."

He didn't stand around to watch it happen because
he knew Joanna would leap into action, and he paced
in front of Hilton Martin's old floral sofa until Gina
walked in.

The confused look on her face almost made him
laugh. Since he'd already used anger as a cover, he
decided slamming his door was a nice touch and he did
that. But the second the hardware of the door clicked,
signaling it was closed, he grabbed Gina's upper arms
and hauled her to him so he could kiss her.

"I don't know how long I'm going to be able to do
this," Gerrick said when he finally managed to pull
away.

Gina only stared at him. "I don't either. I thought you were handling things."

"Barely, but I have a really good idea."

"Oh, yeah?"

"Yeah. How about lunch in my hotel room?"

Gina only giggled. "You can't be serious."

"The hell I'm not!"

"Okay," she said, then started to walk to the door knowing that in order to sneak out at lunch she had to get all her work done this morning, but also thinking that this was the most fun she'd had since college. "You know, we probably should have done this years ago."

"You better believe it."

Though they didn't plan it, Gina knew she would have to leave the building alone and drove to Gerrick's hotel in her own car. She rode the elevator to his room alone, and knocked when she got there though she wasn't sure he had arrived yet because they hadn't co-ordinated their leaving times.

She waited only a few seconds before the door flew open and she was yanked inside and into Gerrick's arms. Because he had already removed his jacket, she didn't wait for him to start removing her clothes. As he kissed her, she worked the buttons of her blouse.

They made love the way Gina suspected any two people with nothing but a lunch hour would make love. Fast and furious. When she finally began to drift back to earth, reality set in and she realized her hair was a mess, her makeup was probably gone and she had fifteen minutes to redress and get back to the office.

But before she could move, Gerrick grabbed her wrist. "Don't even think about it."

She laughed. "We're going to be late... Together."

"No, we're not. I have an out of the office meeting at three-thirty. I told Joanna I wouldn't be returning."

"Oh, good, then just I'll be late."

"Gina, you own part of the company."

"All the more reason to be punctual."

"Are you going to be this crazy the whole way through our marriage?"

Gina pushed herself up on her elbows then rolled to lean against his chest. "Are you complaining?"

"No. But I would like to point out that we never got around to any of that preliminary stuff we were supposed to talk about last night."

"I thought we talked about a hell of a lot."

He shook his head, and combed his fingers through her thick hair. "There's so much we haven't touched on."

Gina realized she had reached the conclusion that they were made for each other on her own. She hadn't needed a deep, dark discussion and neither should he. In some ways she wondered if a forced conversation wouldn't make the relationship seem contrived.

"And maybe we shouldn't touch on it yet."

"I'm not sure I like the sound of that."

"Gerrick, you need to relax, okay? You're going to make both of us nuts by looking for assurances that this is going to last forever. I think you're putting too much pressure on us."

He rolled back on his pillow. "I am going to make us nuts, aren't I?"

"Yes, you are."

"So what do you suggest?"

"That you order me a sandwich while I try to get myself presentable to go back to work."

"I have a better idea."

He gave her a suggestion that sounded like fun, so she followed through and that resulted in their staying in bed for another two hours. Unfortunately, it didn't seem like two hours and Gerrick almost didn't make his meeting. Because it was so late, Gina didn't even go back to work. She also dodged her father when she arrived home. She marched straight to her vanity where she began a serious inventory of what she should take to Gerrick's hotel room. Because she was trying not to be obvious, in the end she only took what she could shove into an oversized purse, and she was very glad she had made that choice when her father again caught her sneaking out through the foyer.

"Going somewhere?"

"Out."

"Just out?"

She smiled. "Just out," she said. Suddenly she realized what all this pacing, waiting for her and ranting was all about. Her father was only looking for confirmation of what he already suspected. Something she wasn't yet permitted to confirm. So she threw him a bone.

"Trust me. When all this comes to light, you are going to be very happy with me."

Her father said, "Hmmm," shook his head, then walked down the hall to his study.

Gina almost laughed out loud. But she didn't. She grabbed the doorknob and propelled herself out into the beautiful Georgia night. Spring was turning out to be her favorite time of the year.

As she expected, when she arrived at Gerrick's hotel room, he pulled her inside again. This time, however, they ordered food because they both realized they hadn't eaten lunch and they were starving.

For about three seconds, Gerrick had considered asking if she would like to go out for dinner, but when she mentioned that she had brought a toothbrush, extra makeup and a black teddy, he didn't bother. Instead, he talked her into changing into the teddy while they waited for the prime rib to arrive, then questioned his intelligence for making that suggestion because she drove him to distraction the entire time they ate. He couldn't wait to get done with dinner so he could ravish her. When they were done eating, he did everything he thought about doing to her and more.

Sated, happier than he had ever been, what he wanted to do was roll over, pull Gina against him and fall asleep, but he knew he couldn't do that. He knew she couldn't stay.

"So when are we going to make this legal?"

She shrugged. "I don't know. I gave my dad a big hint about us tonight and he growled a little, but didn't ask any more questions, basically confirming my theory that he won't interfere until he knows for sure. So, I guess we have to keep the secret as long as we want privacy."

Gerrick laughed. "In other words, we'll announce right before the first kid comes. Or, knowing your dad, if we were smart we wouldn't announce until after the first baby came."

Gina pulled away and studied his face for a second. "What?"

"I… You… Gerrick." She paused and to Gerrick it seemed she drew an overlong breath. Almost as if she were trying to prevent herself from hyperventilating. "You want a baby?"

He frowned. "Not today."

"But eventually?"

"Well, yeah." He paused. "Don't you want kids?"

"It isn't that I don't want kids. I'm not sure I can have kids."

Gerrick felt dizzy. "Do you have a medical problem?"

She laughed and shook her head. "No, silly. But I have a job. Worse, someday I'm going to be running the whole conglomerate. I can't say I'm going to have kids now and then two years down the road, desert them because I'll be too busy running Hilton-Cooper-Martin Foods to give them the time they deserve."

For a good thirty seconds Gerrick only stared at her. "What are you talking about?"

"I'm talking about my responsibility to my family, Gerrick. I have always known I would run this company for my family someday. True, my aunts, uncles and cousins only own enough of the stock to provide them with an income, but it is their income, and making sure that income stays stable is my responsibility."

"I thought it was my responsibility."

"Well, it is. Until you train me..."

"Until I train you?"

"To take over."

Gerrick couldn't help it. He stared at her again. Finally he said, "Gina, no one mentioned any of this to me. No one said that part of my job was to train you."

"Having worked for the company as long as you have, I'm sure my father assumed you understood."

He didn't. Not at all. Not even a little bit. Not just because his discussions with Hilton led him to believe he was the future of the company, and he was the person Hilton believed could keep this company solvent forever. But also because Gina's commitment to him suddenly seemed hollow or maybe incomplete.

"Let me get this straight. You don't want to have kids because you're planning to be an executive for the rest of your life?"

"I guess that's one way to put it, but the truth is that it is more of a family responsibility than a choice."

"You always have a choice."

"I suppose. But mine was made years ago. You had to know that. You were in on the meetings when I was brought in to the company right after college. You heard my father say someday I would take over."

Yes, he had. But he thought things had changed. When Hilton never made any solid effort to promote Gina, he had assumed that Gina didn't want the family mantle.

"I see."

"Gerrick, this doesn't change anything between us."

"Doesn't it?"

"No!"

He shook his head in total disbelief. "I want children, you don't. I want to keep the job that will someday be yours…"

"What are you saying?" Gina's eyes narrowed and Gerrick sensed the storm that was coming. He knew the conclusion to which she jumped and felt the power of her next words before she said them. "My God. You assumed that if you married me, I wouldn't ever want to take over my family's company and you would keep my job."

She was furious, but as far as Gerrick was concerned, she was angry over the little thing. The part of the situation they could resolve quickly and easily if they really wanted to. "This isn't about the job."

"Really." Her facial expression went from angry to sad in mere seconds. "All this time I thought you were the first man who actually wanted me for me, but that's not true, is it? You married me to get me out of the way."

Seeking to comfort her, he soothingly said, "That's ridiculous. When we went to Vegas, neither of us knew your father would have a heart attack. I wouldn't have my job were it not for his getting sick. You can't say I planned this."

"Not this, exactly," Gina said and shifted completely away from him on the bed. "But with me out of the way, who else would my father choose to replace him?" A look of recognition chased away the sadness on Gina's face. "It all makes sense to me now. You didn't know my father would have a heart attack, but that was why you probably felt you had to marry me. Unless you got me out of the way, you knew my father would soon start training me to take over. Then, when we came home and discovered my dad was in the hospital, you probably thought getting married was a wasted effort since you knew you were the only person who could run the company. You even went along when I asked you to leave because you knew my dad would have to bring you back... And he did. The week after you left, he asked you to return. My God, Gerrick, that's why you never called me or wanted a reconciliation... You never wanted me in the first place."

"Gina!" Gerrick said, trying to catch her hand as she leaped from the bed and began snatching up her clothes, but she was quicker than he was.

"Don't!" she said, sounding very much the way she had at the hospital when she asked him to leave. "Don't."

That one word "don't" brought memories of their last breakup to mind. The one where he had heard the stubbornness in her voice and knew there was no changing her mind. Gerrick stepped back, let her grab her clothes, let her dress. He didn't say another word. Not because he didn't want to argue her contention that he had married her to get her job, but because she was proving, again, what he had suspected all along.

She hadn't made a commitment. And though the knowledge didn't stop the pain that ricocheted through him, at least this time Gerrick had an insight as to why she hadn't made a commitment.

She didn't know how. Her experience with men was to expect to be hurt and she held something back, ready, always, to jump out of the relationship before it happened.

The reason their marriage wouldn't work was so obvious it was unbelievable he hadn't seen it before, and so simple it was almost laughable. The man who needed a commitment more than his next breath of air had fallen in love with a woman who didn't know how to make one. And if he stayed with her, if he clung to her because he loved her with a passion that rivaled his fear of losing her, the rest of his life would be spent waiting for the day that she left him for good.

When she got to the door, he said, "Gina."

She didn't even face him.

"I'm really, really sorry."

"Don't try to…"

"I'm not trying to do anything but the right thing." He stopped because his voice faltered. He never wanted anybody, loved anybody the way he loved her. He knew instinctively that he would never feel this way again. It hurt so much that he almost couldn't say the words, but he also couldn't change facts.

"We are so different," he said softly, kindly, struggling to stifle his own pain so she didn't see it and say or do something that would only make matters worse. "That this isn't going to work. I didn't try to get you out of the way. But you can't help jumping to the conclusion that I used you because you're wired not to trust anybody." He paused and drew another breath before he quietly said, "I can't live like this and neither can you."

She faced him and he saw the tears clinging to her eyelids.

"That's why I'm sorry," he continued. "Because it isn't going to work and we both know it."

# Chapter Eight

Numb and angry, Gina drove home. She refused to be fooled or sidetracked by Gerrick's tactic of ending the relationship. He might have been genuinely insulted that she suspected him of using her to become CEO of Hilton-Cooper-Martin Foods, but to someone who had been dodging opportunists all her life Gina knew that the best way to cover one's tracks was to feign outrage. If his injury and insult were sincere, he had picked the absolute worst way to express them. All he had done was make himself look more guilty.

She closed her eyes briefly to stave off the pain of thinking Gerrick had used her, but though she was hurt, though her heart felt as if it were being torn in two, she had to get to the bottom of this. There was a quick, easy way to uncover the truth, and by God she wasn't letting him frighten her or intimidate her into shrinking away from a few simple questions.

When she arrived home, the lights were on but her

father was nowhere around. After a minute of searching she found him in the rose garden by the patio.

Apparently hearing her footfalls, he turned. "Gina?" he said, surprised to see her and probably expecting someone from the household staff.

"Hi."

He took the few steps off the path and onto the brick patio. "Okay, just from the look on your face I can tell there's a problem."

She drew a long breath. "Not just a problem. Something I can't even begin to describe." Fortifying herself, she took another gulp of air. "I have to ask you a few things and I also have to make you promise you won't question why I'm asking."

Her father peered at her, but in keeping with his behavior of late he didn't argue, so Gina plunged in. "When did you and Gerrick start talking about him taking over as CEO?"

"I called him from the hospital in Pennsylvania." Obviously thinking this was going to be a long conversation, Hilton ambled over to the white outdoor table and took a seat on one of the padded chairs. "I know that might sound premature, but you don't have a heart attack without reevaluating your life. I knew very quickly that I wanted to retire."

"You never talked about him becoming CEO before that?" Gina pressed. "Not even as a joke or something?"

"No."

"You didn't ask him to stay when he was offered the job in Maine?"

"No." Her father's face scrunched up in confusion. "Gina, I know you told me not to ask, but what the hell are you getting at?"

Finally seeing that this didn't just affect her, it also affected her father and even Hilton-Cooper-Martin Foods, Gina knew she had to answer that. "I'm trying to figure out if Gerrick set me...us...up."

"Set us up?"

"Oh, come on, Dad. For God's sake. What's the quickest way to get what you want from your employer?"

Hilton chuckled as if that were a ridiculous question. "Do a good job."

Gina shook her head. "No. The quickest way to get what you want is to get *another* job."

"I don't follow."

"I don't see how you can't follow," Gina said, then began to pace because she was starting to think that when it came to Gerrick her father was more gullible than she was. "First, Gerrick made himself your right-hand man. He wasn't exactly indispensable, but when you had your heart attack even Ethan, Josh and I realized Gerrick was the only one who could replace you."

"Which is exactly why I hired him back when I wanted to retire. He *is* the only person who can replace me."

"Yet you didn't offer him anything to stay when he got another job?"

"He was moving on to greener pastures."

"And he never asked for compensation to stay...never hinted that if you gave him a raise or promotion he wouldn't leave?"

"Nope. In fact, he sought my help to get the job." Hilton paused, then caught Gina's hand to stop her pacing. "I didn't wonder why he wanted to move on. The man was born to be number one somewhere. I considered myself lucky to have his help for as long as I did…and it wasn't until I felt *I* needed replacing, which meant our top spot was open, that I enticed him back.''

''You never, ever thought he was after your job?''

Looking at Gina as if she were crazy, Hilton shook his head and Gina swallowed as tingling fear enveloped her. If what her father was telling her was true, and she had no reason to doubt that it was, she had just jumped to the most god-awful conclusion.

She sat on one of the chairs across the table from her father and combed her fingers through her hair. ''Oh, God, this is a mess.''

''Gina,'' her father said slowly, cautiously, ''what the hell happened?''

''I…We…Dad, Gerrick and I got into a big fight tonight because I accused him of trying to keep me from becoming CEO of the company.''

''You what?'' her father gasped.

Gina bounced from her chair and paced again. ''Look at the timing! He's always been in the right place at the right time with you.''

''Because I put him there,'' Hilton said incredulously. ''Everything he has I gave him.''

''Without thought for the fact that I'm supposed to be doing the job he now has?'' Gina challenged.

''Do you want the job he now has?''

''Of course!'' she all but shouted, not understanding why her father was being so obtuse. ''Dad, I've more or less been training to do this for years.''

He shook his head. ''Not really…''

Gina caught the hesitation in his voice and she realized he wasn't the one being obtuse. She was. ''So you did bring Gerrick in to run the company forever?''

Hilton drew a quick breath. ''I brought him in as CEO for as long as he wants to be CEO.''

"And you didn't remember that I'm the person who was supposed to take over?"

"Gina, I don't think you want to take over."

Furious, confused, she spun away, not sure if she should charge into the garden to burn off some of the energy of her anger, or run into the house and weep because it appeared she hadn't simply made a mistake. She had made a huge mistake. Instead, she pivoted to face her father. "How can you say that!"

He caught her hand and forced her to sit again. "Because you've never gone after it. You've never worked for it. Gerrick has. He would fight the devil for the opportunity to do this job. I think he would work for less pay just because the job is so good. And exactly what he wants. He'll do more than keep us solvent for the years he's in charge. This company will thrive and grow under his leadership and that's what we want from the person in charge." He paused and caught her gaze. "Honey, it's more than what we want. It's what we need. Whoever holds that job holds our family's financial future in the palm of his hands. No one's more qualified than Gerrick."

Gina flopped back on her chair, pulling her hair off her face with both hands. "So what the hell am *I* supposed to do now?"

Hilton shook his head. "I don't know. I'm sorry I never talked to you. But the past couple of months you had complained so much about feeling stifled and locked to the company that I thought you were backhandedly telling me you wanted out. At the very least I figured you were saying you didn't want to take over completely."

Fighting hyperventilation, Gina said, "Don't worry about it."

Hilton combed his fingers through his hair. "Look, I know this is probably a bad time to bring this up but I have to know what happened between you and Gerrick. Was your fight bad enough that he's going to quit?"

Gina closed her eyes. "Our fight was bad, but I insulted him personally, not professionally. I'm sure he'll be at his desk tomorrow morning," she said, her head spinning. She wasn't going to run the company. She had insulted the love of her life, and she'd accused him of unforgivable things.

"Well, at least that's good."

"Yeah, that's great." She rose from her seat and began walking to the French doors then changed her mind and headed for the garden path.

"Where are you going?"

"Just for a walk. I need some time to think."

In the morning, with her wits about her and over the shock of her father's admissions, Gina headed directly for Gerrick's office. After an entire night to analyze everything she had come to several conclusions. First, her father was right. If she had really wanted the job as CEO, she would have gone after it. Because she never did, she must not want it. She could concede that to Gerrick this morning.

Second, because her accusations about Gerrick had been unfair, she needed to apologize. Third, if he accepted her apology, she was laying all her cards on the table about their marriage because she had finally figured out the bottom line to that, too. She accused Gerrick of using her because that was what she had been expecting. But Gerrick's assumptions about why she made her accusations proved he was expecting them to fail, too. And the reason they both expected their marriage to fail was that neither one of them had truly made a commitment to it. By keeping the marriage a secret they both had an easy way out.

So, if he accepted her apology, there would be no secret marriage this time. But she didn't think that was going to be a problem. Gerrick desperately needed a commitment. Once she told him her conclusions, she was absolutely positive he would be so relieved he would sweep her into his arms and smother her with kisses.

Come hell or high water, she would walk out of that room wearing his ring and ready to tell Joanna about their Vegas wedding, if only because Joanna would be the first person they saw.

His door was closed, so Gina smiled at Joanna. "Is he in?"

Joanna nodded. Her face was clouded and Gina assumed that meant Gerrick was in a foul mood. "Yes, but I wouldn't go in there if I were you. Hell, I wouldn't go in there if I were Attila the Hun leading an army."

Gina laughed. "Yeah, well, I'll take my chances. Besides, what I have to tell him will put him in a good mood."

"Then go in with my blessing," Joanna said, chuckling as she gestured toward the door.

Gina knocked once but didn't wait for Gerrick to answer. She opened his door and walked inside. To her great dismay he was packing up his desk.

"Gerrick, don't," she said immediately, completely forgetting her rehearsed speech. "I talked with my dad. You were right. I was wrong. He picked you to run the company because he didn't think I wanted the job."

Gerrick didn't say anything. He simply kept packing.

"My dad and I had a long talk. He told me that I

hadn't proven in my tenure that I wanted to be CEO. That I hadn't gone after it.'' She paused to shake her head. "With a few hours to think things through, I see his reasoning. If I didn't work to get the job, I wouldn't work in the job and I wouldn't be the best person to run the company. He thinks you're the best person to run the company and now I agree. So, the job is yours.''

Gerrick paused in his packing, but still didn't say anything.

She didn't blame him for being angry, and the worst of it was she knew this was only the tip of the iceberg. The job was the little half of their problem. But she needed to get the work-related troubles out of the way before she could broach the personal ones.

"Gerrick, I made a mistake. Maybe my dad made a mistake. Maybe he should have talked to me. Maybe I should have discussed all this with him when he hired you back. Who knows? But the bottom line is that we didn't intend to insult you or confuse the issue. Could you please forgive us, so I don't have to tell my sick father that I made you leave when he obviously needs you?''

Gerrick sighed and fell into his chair. "Yeah, you're right. And I also apologize, because hearing you say all that makes me realize I overreacted.''

Internally, she breathed a sigh of relief. "I think we both overreacted because our relationship clouds work issues.''

"Yes. You're right.''

"But I have good news on that front, too.''

Gerrick shook his head. "Don't, Gina. I don't want to hear it.''

"Actually, you just might,'' Gina said, taking the chair in front of his desk though he didn't offer it. "For my whole life I have fought off suitors who didn't really want me, they wanted to get close to my father or the family money or they wanted a job opportunity. Or something. Everybody always seemed to want something.''

"So you've said.''

"I know, but I must not have made my point. I wasn't just explaining that that's been the pattern of my life. I was also saying that in the end, I always discovered that if they can't get what they want, don't get what they want or have to wait for what they want, I'm very expendable. And being expendable makes me afraid. So, I'm cautious. I'm sorry I compared you to them, but if you think about it, it would have been even stranger if I hadn't.''

For that he looked at her. His expression exhibited such confusion that Gina was stunned into silence.

"From where I sit, that doesn't make a whit of sense. Our history together should have told you I wasn't one of them. I didn't need an "in" to your dad's company. I had a job here, which I quit because I had a better one. I didn't want nor need your family's money. After twelve years none of that was clear to you?''

"Yes and no. Gerrick, I was afraid.''

"This time you were afraid. The last time you were overwhelmed with emotion and unable to deal with our marriage. Listen to what you're saying, Gina. Every time the going gets rough, you get going.''

"That's not it at all.''

He drew a long breath and blew it out on a sigh. "I don't want to debate this. Frankly, I completely understand that your life is odd and that makes it very hard for you to trust men.''

Her spirit brightened until she noticed that the coolness never left his eyes. "But?"

"But I'm done. I think it's time to admit we made a mistake and move on...or go back to what we were or something."

"You're just giving up?"

"Gina, I didn't want to try the second time around. You more or less convinced me that we should. Then you proved out what I assumed all along. You're not committed. You might like me." He paused to smile ruefully. "Actually, Gina, I think in your own way you love me. But you are not committed to me. And I can't be in a relationship without a really solid commitment. My past won't allow it. Now, unless you have a work problem, I have to ask you to leave. Josh should be calling with the report of the morning deposits and since I'm not quitting I have to handle that."

Gina rose. She fully expected him to call her back before she made it to his door. He did not. She fully expected that as she walked down the hall, he would grab her arm, spin her around and tell her he hadn't meant any of that. They were too good together, too happy. She couldn't believe he would so easily throw away everything they had. But he never came after her.

She made it to her own suite without even feeling the beginnings of a tear, but once she closed the door and began walking to her desk the realization sunk in that he wouldn't change his mind and every muscle in her body grew limp. She couldn't believe this. Gerrick was the most reasonable man on the face of the earth. And the most understanding. She had been so sure that once she apologized, once she set the record straight, he would simply haul her into his arms and kiss her.

And all would be forgiven.

But nothing was forgiven. They were through.

# *Chapter Nine*

Gina went home early and spent the afternoon pacing in her room, not caring if the cook had her ear to the door or if her dad could hear her back and forth movement across the floor.

She was so confused and distraught she couldn't even cry. But from her father's comments at dinner that evening, Gina knew he thought she was upset because of the argument she had with Gerrick the night before and at least part of her confusion cleared. Unless she wanted her dad to interfere in a predicament that would be horribly embarrassing to both her and Gerrick if it were exposed, she had to pretend nothing was wrong.

She told her dad she had left work early that day because she was sick. The next morning, she went back to her usual routine. She strode through the Hilton-Cooper-Martin Foods building entrance and to her office as if it were an average day and no one said a word to her, least of all Gerrick. In keeping with the typical procedure at Hilton-Cooper-Martin Foods, the Human

Resources director had little contact with the CEO and by the following Wednesday, except for the pain in her heart and the hole in her soul, Gina's life was back to normal.

Unfortunately, Olivia called that afternoon to remind her of the rehearsal for her wedding and Gina remembered she and Gerrick were partners in the bridal party. She almost panicked, but realized that if she panicked everybody would know something was wrong. Everybody from her dad to her secretary would ask questions she not only didn't want to answer, but which would also embarrass Gerrick.

Knowing she had no choice but to pretend she was okay, she smiled at him on Friday evening when he entered the church. "Hi."

"Hi."

"This is going to be a little awkward," she said, motioning up the aisle to where Olivia and Josh stood talking with Josh's mother and Olivia's mother and stepfather.

But Gerrick shook his head. Actually looking as calm as Gina was trying to pretend she was, he said, "Not really. We'll be fine. By the way, I saw my lawyer today."

It surprised her that he would bring that up in a public place, but more than that it hurt. It hurt so much it almost brought tears to her eyes. Almost, but not quite. Knowing she had let the love of her life slip away was bad, and seeing how casual he could be was like rubbing salt into the wound, but if he could be a sophisticated adult about this she could, too.

She forced another smile. "Good. No sense prolonging things."

"My thought exactly," he said, directing her toward Josh and Olivia and the rest of the bridal party.

"I wonder where Savannah and Ethan are?" Gina asked as she and Gerrick approached the altar.

"They're bringing the baby," Olivia said with a laugh. "So I'm guessing they're fighting with the car seat right about now."

"We mastered the car seat long ago," Ethan called, walking up the aisle, holding his six-month-old son Brandon. Beside him his petite wife, Savannah, who was also Gina and Olivia's friend—all three worked together at Hilton-Cooper-Martin Foods at one time— wore a wide grin and toted a diaper bag. Her red hair tumbled around her in a riot of curls.

"Oh!" Olivia cried and scrambled to the back of the church to take the baby from Ethan's arms. "He's so adorable!"

"Yes, he is," Josh agreed, stealing Brandon from Olivia.

"And too cute to be held by a man!" Gina said, taking the baby from Josh's arms.

"Guess again," Gerrick said, snatching him from Gina. "Hey, little guy," he cooed and the toothless child grinned at him. The tufts of hair on his head were bright red like Savannah's, but his blue eyes had already begun to darken and would clearly be brown like Ethan's. "See, he likes me."

"I hate to burst your bubble," Ethan said, as the priest entered, "but he likes everybody." He took the baby from Gerrick and, quiet, content, the little boy eased into the crook of Ethan's arm.

Without delay the rehearsal began, but Gina noticed that Gerrick's gaze seemed to follow the baby wherever he went. Because Gerrick was behind Ethan at the altar,

Gerrick made faces and silly noises as the priest gave instructions to Olivia and Josh. When they filed down the aisle in a trial-run recessional, little Brandon McKenzie giggled over his father's shoulder, playing with Gerrick.

Gina's eyes filled with tears, but again she stopped herself from crying. She wouldn't dwell on the fact that she had blown it with a nice guy who was absolutely perfect for her because the bottom line was *she* had made a mess of everything. He had every reason in the world not to want her and she had no one to blame but herself.

When they reached the back of the church, the priest pronounced them sufficiently prepared for the ceremony, and he left. Because Olivia's mother and stepfather were from out of town, Josh's mother invited them to ride with her to her house for the rehearsal dinner. Within moments they, too, were gone. Olivia and Josh, happy and obviously excited at the prospect of having their own children someday, immediately confiscated the baby.

"He'll be the hit of the rehearsal dinner," Gerrick said, laughing and chucking the baby under his double chin.

"He's the hit of every dinner," Savannah said, then rolled her eyes. "You should see him with the Democratic Party. If baby popularity got people elected Ethan's dad would be president of the United States right now. The only problem is he gets so excited that we can't seem to get him to sleep once we get home."

"That's such a nice problem," Olivia said before she cooed at the baby.

"Tell me that when your first baby is two months

old,'' Ethan said with a laugh, taking Brandon. ''He's gotta ride with us. We're the ones with the car seat.''

''Okay, but dibs on him when we get to Josh's mother's,'' Olivia said, as Josh opened the church door and motioned for her to exit before him.

The future bride and groom joyfully skipped toward Josh's SUV. Carrying the baby and holding Savannah's hand, Ethan led Savannah to their sedan, while whistling Gerrick began walking toward his car.

Everyone was happy but Gina.

Suddenly it was all too much for her, and she knew she had to get the hell out of there. She couldn't take another minute of babies, weddings or men who were happier without her. Why? Because she was tired...

No, what she was was emotionally drained. And why wouldn't she be? She got married, but didn't remember. Her father nearly died, but he got better and when he did he was different—so different she hardly knew how to deal with him. Then she realized she loved Gerrick, but by then he didn't want her anymore.

And the whole time she kept all *her* emotions inside because she didn't want to upset her dad or embarrass Gerrick. Though both of those were noble purposes, the end of her discipline had arrived. She wouldn't be able to hold all her feelings back tonight.

She got into her car, but rather than turn toward her aunt's home and the rehearsal dinner, she headed for her dad's house, her own bedroom and maybe even the comfort of a cup of cocoa. But she also pulled out her cell phone and called Olivia.

''Liv, I'm tired,'' she said, stopping a sob that shuddered up from her chest. ''If I'm going to be halfway decent at the wedding tomorrow I have to beg off on the dinner tonight.''

Olivia sounded disappointed, but agreed that if Gina was tired she should probably go home and rest. Gina disconnected the call and kept a tight rein on herself as she drove through traffic and to her house. But she only made it as far as the foyer before she collapsed on the bottom step and sobbed. Knowing her father was at his sister's house for the rehearsal dinner and the cook was occupied in the kitchen with preparations for tomorrow's wedding, she didn't even try to stop herself. She let herself cry.

Because her crying jag hadn't changed anything, it surprised Gina that she felt better the next day. She felt so good that she jokingly dodged all her father's questions about why she hadn't attended the rehearsal dinner by simply teasing that she had had a headache.

He bought that, so she didn't argue with success. She intended to enjoy Josh and Olivia's wedding. Plus, she was hostess of sorts since the reception was to be held at the Martin mansion and Olivia was dressing in Gina's bedroom. She *needed* to be on top of her game.

Already wearing her plum-colored bridesmaid's dress, Savannah sat on Gina's bed, watching as Olivia stepped into her wedding gown.

"You're sure you're better today?" Olivia asked Gina who was holding open the sequined creation.

"I feel terrific," Gina said, glad she had taken a break the evening before. "I told you I was tired last night."

"When you called, you sounded like you were crying."

Gina laughed as she zipped Olivia's gown. "Last week the cook told my dad I was crying, and what she heard was water running into my bathtub." She turned

Olivia toward the mirror to get her first look at herself. With her blond hair piled high on her head and accented with a sequined tiara, Olivia looked magnificent, regal. The simple sleeveless gown she chose fit snugly in the bodice, then belled out in four large pleats. Sequins studded the neckline and hem.

Olivia pressed her hands to her face and gasped.

Gina smiled. "You look beautiful."

"And *you* look tired," Savannah interjected, talking to Gina.

Olivia nodded. "And you also haven't distracted me from the fact that you sounded like you were crying last night."

"I'm starting to think I better tape my next crying session to hear what I sound like since the only background noise you could have heard was traffic."

"You might not have been crying," Savannah ventured, rising from the bed to arrange the back folds of Olivia's gown. "But you didn't look too good at the rehearsal."

"I told you. I was tired."

Olivia just looked at her. "Right."

"Yeah, right," Savannah agreed.

"You guys keep forgetting my dad almost died and he's facing bypass surgery in a few weeks. If I'm not in top form I think you both should cut me some slack."

Gina knew she said it a little more harshly than she had intended and she immediately apologized. "Sorry."

"No. *We're* sorry," Olivia said, gathering Gina to her for a hug, causing both of their satin dresses to rustle. "This has been a very difficult month for you. We should have been more sympathetic."

"No," Gina said, waving away Olivia's concern. "No. It's not your fault. I'm just tense. Besides, you're not supposed to be preoccupied with me. You're getting married," she said enthusiastically. But the feeling she had had watching everyone leave the rehearsal returned full force. Olivia was getting married. Savannah was married and had a baby. And Gina, well, Gina wasn't anything. She wouldn't be heir apparent CEO of Hilton-Cooper-Martin Foods. Right now she wasn't sure she even had a future at the company. Actually, right now she wasn't sure she *wanted* a future with the company. She didn't have a baby, she didn't have a husband, she didn't even have a potential husband.

"And my dad hired a limo," she continued, forcing excitement into her voice when suddenly all she wanted to do was weep again. "This will be the best day."

"The day you waited for for almost five years," Savannah agreed excitedly. "My gosh! This time last year, you were at the end of your ultimatum. You had quit and were moving to Florida, because Josh hadn't noticed you."

"I know," Olivia said with a grimace, then she burst into giggles. "Thank goodness I didn't stick to it."

"Yeah, thank goodness," Gina agreed, smiling at all the right times as she helped Olivia and her heavy gown down the spiral staircase and to the foyer where her father stood ready to escort them to the limo.

"You look beautiful, Olivia," he said, then hugged her before opening the door.

"Thanks."

"And you girls look great, too!" he said to Gina and Savannah, hugging each of them before ushering them out the door.

Gina accepted both his compliment and his hug, refusing to let herself fall victim to this mood again. But when Olivia walked down the aisle on her stepfather's arm,

Gina realized she would never do this. She would never walk down an aisle. She didn't have a clue what the hell she would do, but it wouldn't be this. She wouldn't run Hilton-Cooper-Martin Foods. She wouldn't get married. Her life stretched before her so barren and empty, she was glad when Olivia and Josh exchanged their vows, and most of the people began to cry, because it was a darned good excuse for Gina to cry, too.

She sobbed through most of the service, and though she controlled herself while posing for the pictures, she began to cry again at the reception when Josh and Olivia danced their first dance as husband and wife.

Savannah sidled up to her and wrapped her arm around her shoulders. "Are you okay?"

Gina waved away her concern. "Weddings make me weepy."

"Very weepy," Savannah said, turning Gina toward the foyer and leading her up the stairs. "Your mascara is running."

"Great."

"We'll fix it," Savannah said, then directed Gina into her bedroom.

"And while we fix it you can tell me what's wrong."

"There's nothing…"

"Something is wrong!" Savannah insisted. "And you're going to let me help you the way I let you help me when Ethan and I were having trouble. So spill it."

Gina drew a long breath. Though she didn't feel at liberty to say anything about her marriage, her life had so many other problems she really didn't need to go there.

"I'll never be CEO of Hilton-Cooper-Martin Foods."

Much to Gina's surprise Savannah laughed. "None

of us will… Except Gerrick, but frankly, Gina, he's the only one of us who is qualified to take that position.''

"So I'm told,'' Gina said, walking into her bathroom where she splashed cold water on her face, careful not to get any on her gown. Glad for the minute alone, she called to Savannah, "It looks like I'll have to start all over again with my makeup.''

But Savannah was at the bathroom door. "That's okay. Take your time. And tell me why you're so upset about not being CEO when you never really seemed to want to be.''

"Because I'm nothing,'' Gina said and unexpectedly started to cry again as that realization washed over her. "My gosh, Savannah, I'm nothing.''

Savannah pulled her into her arms. "Of course, you're something.''

"No, I'm not. All my life I was my father's daughter. Now, he wants a boat.'' She paused to sniff. "I'm being replaced by a boat.''

"Gina you can always go sailing…''

"I don't want to go sailing. I get seasick.''

Savannah laughed. "Lots of us do. But just because you can't ride in his boat…''

Gina shook her head. "Don't you see? My dad and I have 'been' Hilton-Cooper-Martin Foods for almost thirty years. Now he doesn't want to play anymore and I don't fit.''

"Of course you fit.''

"Maybe I don't want to fit.''

"Oh.''

"Yeah, oh.''

"So, what do you want to do?''

"That's just it. I don't know. I spent so much of my

life focused on that darned company that I have no clue who I am or what I want to do.''

''Do you have to be something?''

Gina splashed water on her face again. ''Yes. I'm not Olivia. I'll never be somebody's full-time wife. I'm not you. I can't take over the family bed-and-breakfast and then run it long distance while I raise my child and plan to have more.'' Hearing the emptiness in her life out loud, Gina collapsed to the commode and started to cry again. ''I'm nothing.''

''You're plenty of things,'' Savannah disagreed. ''Most of all, you're somebody Olivia and I care about very much. Josh and Ethan love you, too.'' She paused, drew a breath, then said, ''And Gerrick loves you, too.''

Gina glanced at her friend and realized from Savannah's expression that she knew or had figured out much more than she was saying.

''Actually, he does,'' Gina agreed. ''The truth is that weekend Gerrick and I spent in Vegas wasn't just the little getaway it was supposed to be. We got married....''

Savannah gasped but Gina kept talking so Savannah wouldn't get the wrong impression. ''But the marriage lasted all of twenty-four hours. When he returned from Maine we tried to fix things, but I blew one too many chances with him and now he wants me out of his life for good.''

Looking shell-shocked, Savannah said, ''And now I think we're coming to the real problem.''

''I can't work at Hilton-Cooper-Martin Foods watching him, knowing him, loving him and realizing he doesn't want me.''

''Maybe he...''

Gina shook her head. ''It's over. But the worst of it

isn't that I'll never have him. The worst of it is that I'll someday have to watch while he finds a woman who does fit the bill of his perfect wife. I'll have to watch him date her, then marry her and have their perfect kids.''

''Then I think what you're really saying isn't that you don't belong at Hilton-Cooper-Martin Foods anymore, but that you don't want to be there anymore.''

''Not at all. Not even a little bit.''

''Then I have a suggestion.''

Gina glanced at her.

''Go to Maryland for a few months. Run the bed and breakfast for me.''

''You don't have to…''

Savannah stopped Gina with a laugh. ''You don't even know what I'm about to suggest. In the first place, the whole house needs to be painted, inside and out. So someone's got to hire a subcontractor and supervise the job. In the second, I would like a little rest from being everybody's everything…''

''You're doing fine.''

''I won't argue that,'' Savannah said, ''But sometimes doing so many things can be a little wearing.''

''Well, thank you for the offer, but I'm okay now. I think I just needed to say some of that out loud or something, because I don't feel bad anymore.''

''Are you sure?''

''Yeah, as sure as I'll ever be. I've just got to deal with this.''

''I've never seen you this upset over a breakup before.''

''That's because I've never loved anybody the way I loved Gerrick. But that's okay,'' Gina said, then she blew her nose. "I know this whole mess is my fault. I know I'm to blame. I know I will get over this."

"I think you should go supervise my painting."

"And I think you're a sweet friend, but I'll be fine."

Gina actually believed that until Gerrick asked her to dance. He pulled her into his arms and she felt his strength, saw his smile and wondered how she could have been so foolish as to lose him. Not once, but twice.

"This is really a great wedding."

"Yes, it is," Gina agreed, overwhelmed by his nearness. He was everything she wanted in a man, yet she managed to screw up and now he didn't want her anymore.

"And Josh and Olivia look very happy."

"They are very happy," Gina said. "Olivia had a crush on him for over four years. Even now none of us is really sure what she did to get him to notice her."

"Desperate people do desperate things," Gerrick said and Gina felt herself crumble inside. She knew he was talking about himself. She suspected he was admitting that desperation drove him to marry her in Vegas.

"Look, don't think about that, okay?" Gerrick said, tightening his hold on her. "We'll be fine. I've survived worse mistakes and it sounds like you have, too. The thing is we both need to relax and get on with the rest of our lives."

"Yes, I know," Gina agreed, but she finally realized that was the problem. Not that she would have to watch him find the woman of his dreams, court her and marry her...but that he could do it. He wasn't paralyzed like she was. He wasn't stricken the way she was. He was up and running again.

The song ended and Gina and Gerrick parted company. Gina walked to the bar pretending to get a drink, but covertly watched as he asked another woman to dance. Studying him as he laughed and chatted, waltzing around the dance floor, she confirmed everything she had suspected.

He might have loved her. He might still love her. But he was fully capable of getting on with the rest of his life and planned to do so. Unless Gina wanted to be in the background while he did, she had to get the hell out of here.

Racing away from the bar she found Savannah. "I've decided I'm going to do that bed and breakfast thing," she said, leading Savannah up the steps again.

"Good," Savannah said, obviously confused about why they had to go upstairs to talk about this.

"I'm leaving tonight. Actually, I'm leaving now," she said, stepping out of her dress as Savannah closed her bedroom door. "Do I need a key or something?"

Stunned, Savannah only gaped at her.

Gina pulled a lightweight top over her head. "Do I need a key?" she asked again.

"No," Savannah said, incredulously watching Gina dress. "I have four friends who take turns house-sitting. If there is no guest, no one will be there, but since it's Saturday night I'm sure there's a guest."

"Give me your friends' names and phone numbers anyway." She handed Savannah a pen and pencil. Savannah began scribbling as Gina packed a small suitcase. "Then I've got to smuggle myself out."

Savannah gaped at her again. "You're serious."

"Absolutely."

"Okay," Savannah said, handing her the paper and pen. "Here are the names and numbers of my friends. They'll help you with anything you need."

"Good."

Gina started toward the door, but Savannah stopped her. "They'll help you with *anything* you need," she repeated. "Anything. Don't hesitate to ask. They pulled me through a lot of tough times after my parents died."

"They sound like good friends."

"They are. They'll help you through this."

"Good," Gina said, then kissed Savannah's cheek. "Before you go home tonight, explain some of this to my dad." She paused, caught Savannah's gaze. "Leave out the messy parts. Make it look like this is a career choice. Tell him I'll be home the week of his surgery, but I'll probably go back to Maryland after that. Make it sound like a business decision. Make me sound smart."

Savannah sighed. "You are smart."

"So everybody keeps telling me," Gina said then headed for the back stairs and the back door, which led to the garage. To date, she had absolutely no confirmation of her intelligence but she did believe she was getting very good at subterfuge.

"Has anybody seen Gina?"

Hilton Martin asked the question as he walked over to the cluster of friends in which Gerrick stood. With Josh and Olivia now married, and Savannah and Ethan already married parents, it hadn't escaped Gerrick's notice that he was the only one not committed to someone. Technically, he was married, but that would be over in a matter of weeks.

The thought tweaked his heart but he ignored the pain. Gina might have looked exceptionally beautiful. She truly might be the love of his life. But they couldn't get along. They had personalities that didn't mesh. No matter how much he wanted them to.

"No. I haven't seen Gina," Olivia said, glancing around curiously. "Now that you mention it, I haven't seen her in over an hour."

"Neither have I," Josh muttered as he, too, looked around, obviously seeking her out in the crowd of wedding guests.

"It's been at least an hour since she and I danced," Hilton said. "I saw her once or twice after that, then poof. She was gone."

"I'm sure she's around somewhere," Ethan said, but Gerrick saw Savannah squirm uncomfortably. Ethan turned to his wife. "You know something you're not telling."

"Actually, Hilton," Savannah said, "I was supposed to have a private conversation with you about this later…"

Hilton's eyes narrowed. "About what?"

"Well…" she glanced at Gerrick. "Well…"

"Well what?" Hilton demanded. "What has Gina done now?"

"Gina hasn't done anything," Savannah hastily assured him. "It's just… Well… Actually, she did do something. My bed-and-breakfast needs to be painted so she agreed to go to Maryland for me and hire the subcontractor and supervise the job."

Gerrick, Olivia, Josh and Hilton only stared at Savannah. Ethan said, "She went *tonight?*"

Obviously uncomfortable, Savannah said, "Yeah."

"Why the hell would she go paint your house in the middle of a wedding?" Hilton demanded, losing his temper.

Gerrick almost panicked. Not just because Hilton was a little too sick be to getting this upset or because he seemed unreasonably angry with Gina, but because Gerrick, like Hilton, knew something was wrong. Something had to be terribly wrong for Gina to leave in the middle of her best friend's wedding.

Refusing to jump to a conclusion, he said, "I'm sure there's an explanation."

"Yeah, there is," Savannah agreed. "And, frankly, Gerrick if anybody should give it, I've decided it should be you."

"She left because of me?" Gerrick said and again felt the horrible, overwhelming sense that something was terribly wrong.

Savannah gaped at him. "You just don't get it, do you? You hurt her."

"Don't tell me you fired her in retaliation for her firing you when I was in the hospital," Hilton all but roared and Gerrick quickly faced him. With his own fears crowding in on him, causing him intense worry about Gina, he didn't need for Hilton to have another heart attack.

"Hilton, calm down..."

"I will not calm down! You hurt my little girl!"

"I didn't hurt her. At least not intentionally," Gerrick said, suddenly getting a new picture of everything that had happened between him and Gina. Of course, he knew he had hurt her, but until this moment her pain was something like an abstract thing. Knowing she had left her best friend's wedding because she was distraught, Gerrick began to realize how much he had wounded her.

"Oh, no?" Hilton demanded, nose to nose with Gerrick now. "Then would you mind telling me how you can unintentionally hurt someone and not give a damn?"

"I do give a damn," Gerrick said and felt the weight

of it the whole way to his soul. *He'd hurt her.* He couldn't believe he had been such a fool that he didn't recognize what that meant. He had seen her sadness when her last boyfriend left her, and he wanted to kill the guy, but he turned around and did the same thing.

"Gerrick, you have about thirty seconds to tell me this story, then I'm going into the den for my gun…"

"All right," Gerrick said, combing his fingers through his hair, knowing he had to give an abbreviated version and get the hell out of here to find Gina. He didn't have a clue of how, but he fully intended to fix this. "The long and short of it is, Gina and I went to Vegas the weekend of your heart attack. We went there to celebrate my new job, and ended up getting married, but…"

Hilton's face turned white. He staggered. *"You what?"*

# Chapter Ten

"Gina and I got married in Vegas," Gerrick repeated, then took a cautious step back. "We thought you knew."

"No! I did not know!" Hilton thundered.

"It seemed like you knew," Gerrick said, torn between concern for Hilton and running after Gina. He didn't know how he hadn't realized how much he had hurt her, except that she always seemed so strong. She *was* strong. But he had witnessed her vulnerability. He knew the truth. Yet he had still hurt her.

"I didn't know!" Hilton glared at Olivia, Ethan and Josh. "Did you know?"

Olivia nodded miserably. "I knew."

"I guessed," Josh said, grimacing.

"I suspected," Ethan said.

Savannah squirmed uncomfortably. "She told me tonight."

"Well, thank you all very much."

Savannah placed her hand on Hilton's forearm. "I

was going to tell you. She asked me to explain this to you after the wedding.''

"Why didn't *she* tell me?''

"I think that was my fault,'' Gerrick began but Hilton interrupted him.

"You think that was your fault,'' he mocked, then took a sharp breath.

Gerrick turned to Ethan. "Get Dr. Brown!''

"Don't you go mothering me, you daughter stealer!'' Hilton said, seemingly regaining his strength to fight the battle.

"Hilton, I'm not a daughter stealer. Gina actually proposed to me.''

"That doesn't make one whit of sense.''

Remembering the exact moment and the circumstances, Gerrick grimaced. "It made a lot of sense at the time.''

"No, it doesn't, Gerrick! For God's sake! If she was the one who proposed and you accepted, you wouldn't be acting like an ass right now, and Gina,'' he paused as if remembering something, and when he spoke again his voice quivered. "And Gina wouldn't have spent the past month trying to get you to notice her…'' He caught Gerrick's gaze and Gerrick saw not the eyes of a businessman or even the eyes of a friend, but the tear-filled, confused eyes of a father. "Why would you make her jump through hoops? Make her beg you to love her?''

Gerrick felt a ton of weight being added to the guilt he already felt. "I didn't make her beg…''

"Really?''

But Gerrick knew that wasn't true. After he returned from Maine she had done everything but seduce him to get another chance. Actually, she had even seduced him.

He looked at Hilton who appeared to be on the verge

of another heart attack or at least desperately in need of rest, and thought of Gina driving to Maryland in the middle of the night. He knew Gina could handle herself for a few hours, but he didn't want her to have to. He also knew she would kill him if he let anything happen to her father. Still, he wasn't the only person on the patio concerned for Hilton. But he was the only person who loved Gina the way he did.

He caught Olivia's hand. "Can you guys handle this? I can't stay another minute. I have to go find her."

Because Savannah didn't know what route Gina had taken north, Gerrick set out on the most logical one. Unfortunately, in almost twelve hours of driving, he never found her. Given that she had at least an hour head start, Gerrick wasn't surprised. When he turned off Route 15 and into Thurmont, Maryland the next morning, he wasn't even tired. Telephone calls from Josh and Ethan reporting that Hilton was fine and continued to be fine, kept him more than alert, but so did his need to make things right with Gina.

Several times he had tried to reach her on her cell phone, but it only rang and rang, an indication that she could have forgotten to take it or could be ignoring him. He didn't blame her. In fact, he wasn't even sure how he would get her to talk to him once he found her.

When he arrived at the bed-and-breakfast, the doors were locked and no one answered when he knocked. Because Savannah had told him Gina might have to go to the home of one of her friends to get keys, he sat on the porch to wait for her.

When she arrived, she was flanked by four young women. Wearing jeans and a form-fitting top, she looked young and beautiful. Happy and healthy. And not at all like a woman who had driven a thousand miles to get away from him because he hurt her.

"You don't seem as hurt as Savannah said."

"Yeah, well, you don't seem like a guy who would give a damn anyway, so what difference does it make?"

He rose from the rocker. "I do give a damn. I was so worried I didn't even stop home to change." He glanced down at himself. "I drove a thousand miles in a tuxedo…"

"Well, now you can drive a thousand miles back, because I don't want you here."

The four women at her side appeared to surround her. Not one of them appeared to be older than twenty-three, but Gerrick got the sense that if they needed to they could be very strong and he could be in deep trouble.

"Can we talk somewhere alone?"

"I've vowed never to be alone with you again."

"That's going to make it very hard to sleep together," Gerrick said only half joking. Sometimes it didn't hurt to cut right to the heart of the issue and avoid all the nonsense that sometimes clouded it.

"Hah! As if I would sleep with you ever again!"

"Gina, we're still married."

"Yeah, but now *neither* of us wants to be married. So you can just hit the road. This time, I'm holding my ground. We made a mistake, let's just correct it."

Seeing his quick fix had failed, Gerrick combed his fingers through his hair. "All right. Look, I know I've been a jerk. But you also know I had my reasons."

"You were afraid of getting hurt so you hurt me first."

"I hurt myself, too."

"Then you're even dumber than I thought." She turned away from him and motioned to her friends to start walking again. "Now, if you'll excuse us, we're going to write a bid proposal to get this house painted."

Gina and her new friends walked up the steps and then past him on the porch. The first woman in line, a tall, willowy blonde, turned to him and said, "I'm Lindsay. I'm in law school," ostensibly to explain how they could write the bid, but Gerrick got the sense that her words doubled as a threat.

He took two steps back. Letting them pass. When they were in the house, he again sat on the old rocker.

He didn't have a clue what he was going to do, but he also knew he had made this mess and wasn't leaving without Gina. He sat for about two minutes before one of the young women joined him on the porch. She actually handed him a cup of coffee and Gerrick only stared at her.

She smiled. "I'm Becki," she said. "Mandi's twin."

"Ah, then Mandi is the other redhead," Gerrick said. He sipped the coffee. "That leaves only the brunette."

"That's Andi."

He nodded toward his cup. "Thanks for the coffee."

"You're welcome."

A few seconds of silence passed as Becki sat on the porch rail across from his rocker. "I've known Gina exactly three hours. Found her on that chair when I arrived this morning to get ready for the guests we have coming tonight."

"Was she okay?"

"She looks okay. She has a very strong façade that makes everybody think she's made of granite or something. I think my sister, my friends and I are going to make her our new idol."

Gerrick laughed.

"But inside," Becki continued, pointing to her chest

at the place her heart would be. "I think she's very soft."

Gerrick studied the angelic face of Gina's newfound friend. She had porcelain skin and emotional blue eyes, and he recognized that if anybody could see into another person's soul, it was probably Becki.

Gerrick glanced down at his shoes. "I didn't realize that until yesterday."

Her head tilted to the right, Becki peered at him. "How could you miss it?"

"Focused on myself," Gerrick said, admitting the truth aloud for the first time. "My parents abandoned me. The aunt and uncle who raised me were killed right after I graduated from college…"

"And rather than see Gina as being the person who could love you, you decided she was the person who would hurt you."

Gerrick narrowed his gaze at her. "How do you know?"

"Only people you really love have the power to hurt you. So if you know she can hurt you, that also has to mean that you love her very much."

Gerrick only stared at her.

Becki laughed. "It's not a gift. It's a fact of life. But it's also true that she must love you very much or she wouldn't be hurt, either."

"So things aren't hopeless?"

Becki rose and headed for the door. "Not hardly. You might have to work a bit to push beyond the façade, but obviously you've done it before at least once."

Gerrick grimaced. "You wouldn't happen to have a bottle of champagne around here anywhere?"

"No alcohol!" Becki said with a laugh and opened the front door. "You do this the fair way this time."

Gerrick followed her into the living room where Gina and company had their heads together talking paint.

"Gina, I'm not taking *no* for an answer."

Gina looked up, her expression completely blank. "Excuse me?"

"I'm not taking *no* for an answer. You and I need to talk."

"Our lawyers need to talk," Gina countered. "Gerrick, do you realize we never signed a prenuptial agreement?"

Lindsay, the tall, willowy blonde, smirked at him.

"We didn't need a prenuptial agreement."

"You think I'm going to sit by and let you take half my share of Hilton-Cooper-Martin Foods?"

"I don't want half of your share of Hilton-Cooper-Martin Foods. I don't need it. I get to run the place and earn a salary. Your dividends can be yours," he said, glaring at Lindsay, who looked like she would be absolutely lethal in the courtroom. "If you want an after-the-fact agreement about our money, I'll sign it, but I'm not giving you a divorce."

"Gerrick…"

"No, listen to me, Gina. I finally figured out what went wrong."

"I thought we already knew what went wrong. That I hadn't made a commitment and you couldn't sit around and wait for me to hurt you so you hurt me first."

"That's almost it, but not quite. The truth is, Gina," Gerrick said and started to laugh, suddenly overwhelmed with the relief of talking to her normally. He didn't have to be guarded or careful. He didn't have to hide his past or worry about his future. She knew him. She knew everything about him. But she loved him anyway. She loved him enough that she took the drastic step of leaving home rather than face every day without him. "I finally realized last night that I was the one who hurt you, which means I was the one who didn't make the commitment."

"Okay, now you're making all of us want to have you committed…"

"I *am* committed."

"I'm talking about committed to an insane asylum."

Gerrick laughed again. He loved her sense of humor. He loved *her*. And she loved him. The more she tried to hide it the more obvious it became to him. He laughed loud and long and Gina and her friends stared at him.

But Gina also asked her friends to leave.

"Gerrick, are you all right?"

"I'm the best I have been in thirty-four years," he said, then wrapped his arms around her waist. "I love you," he said, in a tone of voice that staggered Gina with its sincerity.

"Gerrick, I really don't want to go down this road again."

"Neither do I. I think we need to go down another road."

"I mean it," Gina said. "If you don't start talking sense I'm going to call my dad."

"Ouch. Don't do that. He's already so angry with me I think I may get fired."

"What did you do?"

"Hurt his little girl."

Gina grimaced.

"Savannah told him?"

"Actually, we all came clean. Josh and Olivia knew we were married. Ethan suspected. I understand you told Savannah."

"He's going to kill me."

"No, he's going to kill me...because I hurt you, but I think that if we came home happy, everyone would live."

At that, Gina stepped out of his arms. "Gerrick, we tried this twice. It didn't work. I don't want to get hurt again."

"Is that what I sounded like?"

Gina didn't have time to think about her answer and replied honestly, "Yes. Yeah. I guess it is."

"I'm so sorry. I didn't intend to hurt you, but once I realized how hurt you were I suddenly saw that if I could hurt you and walk away, then I was the one who was in the wrong."

"You have your reasons. It's okay, Gerrick." Refusing to stay around until he talked her into weakening, Gina turned and began walking out of the room. He sounded different, sincere, but he hurt her so much, she couldn't take the risk again.

"No. It's not okay," he called desperately, causing her to stop. "I don't really think my excuses hold water anymore. I think being careful saved me. I'm sure it saved me a great deal of heartache in my life. But being careful doesn't have any place in a marriage. And I'm the one who has to change. You're perfect just the way you are."

His words hit her in the heart, because she knew that he loved her for herself and the experience was so unique it staggered her. But to hear he was willing to risk being hurt by dropping his protective walls for her took her breath, as well as the last of her resistance, away.

"If you would have me," Gerrick said, slowly approaching her from behind. "This time I would trust you." He took another step. "This time I would let myself need you." He took the final step. "This time I would love you the way you deserve to be loved."

Gina wanted to turn. She really did. His words made her long to turn into his arms… But she couldn't.

So he reached out and turned her. "This time I'm asking *you* to marry *me*."

She would have collapsed into his waiting arms, but what he said sank in and she stopped her natural reaction and peered at him. "You didn't ask me the last time?"

"No. You asked me."

Her head dipped in defeat. "Damn. This is even more embarrassing than I thought."

"But think of the great story it makes for our grandkids," he said, then pulled out her wedding ring from the breast pocket of his jacket. Because he told her he hadn't gone home, but had immediately left Atlanta to look for her, she knew he had carried the ring with him. The fact that he couldn't seem to be separated from it nearly brought her to tears.

"You can have this and we can laugh and tease and dodge the slings and arrows generated by our first wedding… Or we can pretend the first wedding didn't happen and start all over again."

She thought of her dad. She thought of how he would probably like to walk her down the aisle. Then she thought of Gerrick and how much he really needed her and how much he needed to know she loved him, believed him and wouldn't ever doubt him again.

She took the ring.

"You're not getting this back, buster," she said, sliding the ring onto her third finger left hand. "I'm not giving you another chance to change your mind."

"This time I won't," he vowed.

"I know," she said, stretching on her toes to kiss him, but he caught her around the waist and pulled her up for a long, passionate kiss that somehow felt different.

"Do that again."

He did. This time more slowly. Their tongues twined with delicious indolence. Her breasts pressed against his chest. His fingers tangled loosely and lovingly into her hair. She realized his desperation was gone.

"You *are* mine," she breathed incredulously as he let her slide back to the floor.

He nodded. "I am yours."

"Even the way you kissed me changed."

"I feel a hundred percent different. Like I've never felt before. It's like I've been set free."

"Maybe you have."

He nodded. "Maybe I have." He paused. "But you haven't. You do realize that you're not going to get my job. And we have to find a house. And I still want kids. I'll negotiate numbers and nannies, but I want kids and you're still an executive…"

"I don't think so," Gina said, then stretched to kiss him again. "Remember what my dad said when toasting your return from Maine about knowing when it was time to leave and going?"

He nodded.

"Well, I'm going. You run the company. I want to raise our kids and take care of my dad."

"Your dad is fine," Gerrick said. "He was a bit upset

last night, but Dr. Brown was at the wedding and Josh and Ethan called with hourly updates."

Gina's eyes widened with fear. "Something happened to my dad?"

"It all revolves around him wanting to kill me and has little to do with his actual physical health. Though I think he'll rest a lot easier when we get home, tell him we're staying married and offer him grandkids."

"Grandkids!" Gina said, clapping her hands. "Grandkids! Why didn't we think of this before!"

"Think of what?"

"Grandkids will be a much better way for him to pick up women than a boat or a dating service!"

She laughed with glee and Gerrick joined her. "Okay, here's another story for our own grandkids... How we had their parents to keep their great grandfather off the street."

"And out of the dating services."

Knowing they needed to get home to ease Gina's father's worries, Gina and Gerrick said goodbye to Savannah's friends and walked to the street where they had parked their respective cars.

"I have a better idea," Gerrick said, opening his passenger side door and offering Gina entry. "Let's leave your car. We can send someone to pick it up later."

"But..."

"Maybe Savannah's friends would want to drive it down to get a chance to visit her..."

"But..."

"Gina, I'm not a person who believes in luck or omens. But the Sunday we returned from Vegas, if we hadn't had two cars to drive home from that bar where we met Friday night, we would have met Ethan as a married couple. You would have been forced to tell your dad, and none of this commitment stuff would have happened. Are you willing to risk it a second time?''

She jumped into his car. ''We'll get Savannah's friends to drive my car to Georgia.''

He bent into the car and kissed her. ''My thought exactly.''

\* \* \* \* \*

# SILHOUETTE *Romance*™

**Lost siblings, secret worlds,
tender seduction—live the fantasy in...**

# A TALE OF THE SEA

**Separated and hidden since childhood,
Phoebe, Kai, Saegar and Thalassa
must reunite in order to safeguard
their underwater kingdom.
But who will protect *them*...?**

*Look for these titles wherever
Silhouette books are sold!*

*Silhouette*®

*Where love comes alive*™

Visit Silhouette at www.eHarlequin.com          SRTOS

If you enjoyed what you just read,
then we've got an offer you can't resist!

# Take 2 bestselling love stories FREE!

# Plus get a FREE surprise gift!

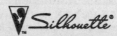

# COMING NEXT MONTH

**#1606 THE PRINCESS HAS AMNESIA!—Patricia Thayer**
*Crown and Glory*
Who was the beauty that fell from the sky—right into former FBI
agent Jake Sanderstone's mountain refuge? Ana was bossy, stricken
with amnesia and…a princess! But when her memory came flooding
back, would she let go of love and return to royalty?

**#1607 FALLING FOR THE SHEIK—Carol Grace**
A bad fall at a ski run left Rahman Harun helpless—and he hated it.
But when private nurse Amanda Reston entered his family's cabin, the
strong sheik decided he needed her tender, loving care! Her nurturing
nature healed his body. Could she also heal his wounded heart?

**#1608 IN DEEP WATERS—Melissa McClone**
*A Tale of the Sea*
Kai Waterton had been warned to stay away from the sea. That didn't stop
her from heading an expedition to find a sunken ship—or falling for
single dad and salvager Ben Mendoza! But what would happen to their
budding romance when the mysteries of her past were uncovered…?

**#1609 THE LAST VIRGIN IN OAKDALE—Wendy Warren**
Be Eleanor's "love tutor"? Cole Sullivan was shocked. His once-shy
buddy in high school, now a tenderhearted veterinarian, had chosen her
former crush to initiate her in the art of lovemaking. But Cole found
himself with second thoughts…and third thoughts…all about Eleanor!

**#1610 BOUGHT BY THE BILLIONAIRE—Myrna Mackenzie**
*The Wedding Auction*
When Maggie Todd entered herself in a charity auction, she'd never
anticipated being asked to pretend to be royalty! As the wealthy charmer
Ethan Bennington tutored the unsophisticated yet enticing Maggie in
becoming a "lady," he found he wanted her to become *his* lady….

**#1611 FIRST YOU KISS 100 MEN…—Carolyn Greene**
Being the Mystery Kisser was easy for columnist Julie Fasano—at
first. Anonymously writing about kissing men got more difficult when
she met up with investigator Hunter Matthews. Hunter was determined
to find the kisser's identity—would he discover her little secret as *they*
shared kisses?